CLOWNS OF TERROR
AN EVIL ANTHOLOGY

OTHER LIVING DEAD PRESS BOOKS

THE TURNING: A STORY OF THE LIVING DEAD * MEN OF PERDITION
THE DEAD OF SPACE BOOK 1 & 2 * THE BABYLONIAN CURSE
PLAYING GOD: A ZOMBIE NOVEL * THE JUNKYARD
SUPERHEROES VS. ZOMBIES
PLANET OF THE DEAD: Vol 1-3 * THE HAUNTED THEATRE
ZOMBIES IN OUR HOMETOWN * ATOMIC ZOMBIES
UNITED STATES OF ARMAGEDDON
THE Z WORD * REVIEWS OF THE DEAD
NIGHT OF THE WOLF: A WEREWOLF ANTHOLOGY
JUST BEFORE NIGHT: A ZOMBIE ANTHOLOGY
THE BOOK OF HORROR 1 & 2
THE WAR AGAINST THEM: A ZOMBIE NOVEL
CHILDREN OF THE VOID * DARK DREAMS
BLOOD RAGE & DEAD RAGE (BOOK 1& 2 OF THE RAGE VIRUS SERIES)
DEAD MOURNING: A ZOMBIE HORROR STORY
BOOK OF THE DEAD: A ZOMBIE ANTHOLOGY VOLUME 1-6
LOVE IS DEAD: A ZOMBIE ANTHOLOGY
ETERNAL NIGHT: A VAMPIRE ANTHOLOGY
END OF DAYS: AN APOCALYPTIC ANTHOLOGY VOLUME 1-5
THE ZOMBIE IN THE BASEMENT (FOR ALL AGES)
DEAD WORLDS: UNDEAD STORIES VOLUMES 1-7
FAMILY OF THE DEAD * REVOLUTION OF THE DEAD
KINGDOM OF THE DEAD * DEAD HISTORY: Vol 1 &2
THE MONSTER UNDER THE BED * DEAD THINGS
DEAD TALES: SHORT STORIES TO DIE FOR
ROAD KILL: A ZOMBIE TALE * DEADFREEZE * DEADFALL
SOUL EATER * THE DARK * RISE OF THE DEAD
DEAD END: A ZOMBIE NOVEL * VISIONS OF THE DEAD
THE CHRONICLES OF JACK PRIMUS: Vol 1&2
BOOK OF CANNIBALS VOLUME 2 * CHRISTMAS IS DEAD…AGAIN
EMAILS OF THE DEAD * CHILDREN OF THE DEAD
TALES OF THE DEAD * TALES OF BIGFOOT
NOVELLAS OF THE DEAD * ETERNAL AFTERMATH 1 & 2
TEN SILLY ZOMBIES JUMPING ON THE BED
ZOMBIES ARE COOL
ZOMBIES ARE PEOPLE TOO

THE DEADWATER SERIES

DEADWATER * DEADWATER: Expanded Edition
DEADRAIN * DEADCITY * DEADWAVE * DEAD HARVEST
DEAD UNION * DEAD VALLEY * DEAD TOWN/ HOMEWARD BOUND
DEAD GRAVE * DEAD SALVATION * DEAD ARMY

CLOWNS OF TERROR
AN EVIL ANTHOLOGY

EDITED BY
ANTHONY GIANGREGORIO

Table of Contents

FOREWORD

Though not many people actually suffer from the irrational phobia called Coulrophobia (fear of clowns) the fact is that there are a hell of a lot more people who simply don't like them.

And for good reason. Clowns are just plain freaky. Perhaps it's because the man or woman behind all that makeup is hidden from us, and though we might think their benevolent, for all we know they're an escaped axe murderer or something just as sinister.

Did you know that there are circuses that have held workshops to help some of their patrons get over their fear of clowns by letting them sit in and watch while the stage performers—the clowns—put on their makeup and transform themselves from ordinary people into harlequins?

In Sarasota, Florida, in 2006, there was such a loathing for clowns that it became criminal when dozens of fiberglass clown statues were defaced, their limbs broken, heads lopped off, spray-painted, and two were stolen, never to be seen again. One can only wonder what horrors those poor statues suffered before finally being destroyed. These statues were part of a public art exhibition named "Clowning Around Town" which was also an homage to the city's history as a winter haven for traveling circuses.

But what about the children? The reason we think of clowns in the first place? Well, truth be told, most kids don't like clowns either. In 2008, at the University of Sheffield, England, a survey of two-hundred and fifty children the ages of four and sixteen found that most children not only disliked clowns, but that they feared them, too, and don't think they're funny at all.

Though clowns are trying to be funny and happy, the very image of what we should think 'fun' is, somewhere down the line the supposedly jolly figure has become evil personified, weighed down by both fear and sadness.

So when did clowns become so dark?

Maybe the truth is that they've always have been that way.

Clowns are pranksters, jesters, jokers, and tricksters, and they have in fact been around for ages. They've appeared in most cultures, such as Pygmy clowns that entertained Egyptian pharaohs in 2500 BC, or in ancient imperial China, where a court clown called a *YuSze* was the only guy who could poke holes in Emperor Qin Shih Huang's plan to paint the Great Wall of China. Hopi Native Americans had a tradition of clown-like characters who interrupted serious dance rituals with crazy antics. Ancient Rome's clown was a fool called a *stupidus,* and the court jesters of medieval Europe were a sanctioned way for the lower classes to poke fun at the people in charge, and the list goes on with Western Europe and Britain added in the mix as well.

So if you take all of this into account, then the clown is a mischief maker, a buffoon there to make people laugh.

But then where did the dark side come from? I mean, pranks are one thing, but where did the homicidal clown come from that we see today in movies and books?

Well, one place might be with Charles Dickens, who may have helped in swaying the popular image of the innocuous clown and make it a scarier figure. You might even say that Dickens created the scary clown. Dickens' edited version of Grimaldi's memoirs was so popular—of a character that was dark and troubled, despite supposedly being happy—that his new creation couldn't help but stick in the minds of his London audience. Later, in 1836, he wrote "The Pickwick Papers" as well.

Then soon after in Paris, came Jean-Gaspard Deburau's Pierrot, a clown with a face painted white, red lips, black eyebrows, whose silent gestures delighted French audiences.

Deburau was so popular in fact that even without his makeup he was recognized.

But in 1836, Deburau killed a boy with his walking stick after the youth yelled insults at him on the street—he was ultimately acquitted of the murder however. So the two most popular clowns of the early modern era were both troubled men underneath their face-paint.

So what is it that actually makes someone fearful of clowns to the point that they can barely stay in the presence of one?

Some believe it emanates from a childhood experience. For a small child, a clown can be quite an imposing figure, this, added with the noise and hectic environment of a party or a circus, can be quite overwhelming to a young child. Then turn this into something that is frightening, and at such a young age the trauma can follow the child all the way into adulthood, where there is always a lingering and unsettling fear of clowns.

Even without all this, the modern day clown has morphed into something terrifying. Whether you're referring to the homicidal maniac known as 'The Joker' in the Batman comics, or in Stephen Kings novel 'It,' where a malevolent clown named 'Pennywise' is stealing children, the clown for this century is a far cry from what it once was.

Clowns are often an easy character to use in horror movies, where budgets are small and usually the talent is even smaller, but even the lowest 'D' movie can afford some white pancake makeup and a clown suit, then add copious amounts of blood and a few killing instruments, most notably a knife, and you have a recipe for horror that in most cases should not fail, especially when studios are targeting their audience's childhood fear of clowns.

In many ways, we all suffer from Coulrophobia just a little, for who amongst us can stand face to face with a tall, daunting figure in loud, colorful clothes that stands out from the norm, with a face hidden behind makeup to the point that you have no idea what they're thinking, as their facial expressions are entirely hidden, and only their eyes give any true meaning to who they really are.

AG

POSTPARTUM

R.P.STEEVES

Perhaps in retrospect, the circus theme was not the best choice. After all, the terror that had followed from that decision would haunt Lana for ages to come.

It had been Max's idea, in the end, though he had made the decision in his typical passive-aggressive fashion. Lana had decided on a simple gray, more of a stone color than charcoal, of course. No need to make the nursery a somber place—though that, in the end, would have been preferable to terrifying. She'd also considered a few adornments—a tree or two with a smattering of tasteful birds—but Lana had never even broached the idea of a gaudy theme. There would be no cheery school buses or anthropomorphic alphabets in her daughter's room.

But Max, true to form, had made a unilateral decision. He had purchased the neon colors—pink was bad enough; she loathed the ironclad traditions of gendered colors, but the fluorescent orange was eye-melting—and an inordinate amount of peel-and-stick caricatures of the circus variety: lions and acrobats, ringmasters, and bears on unicycles.

And clowns.

He had made the purchase of the offending items without her knowledge or consent. They'd discussed the overall look of their firstborn's first room only briefly but Lana had, foolishly, in retrospect, assumed that, as the primary decorative force in the couple—not to mention the mother-to-be and individual who would disgorge the child into the world after a painful period of bearing and pushing—that she would be the one to make the final decision.

Now, of course, she regretted not having put her size five foot down.

She had been attending her baby shower—primarily consisting of Max's relatives, as most of Lana's family and friends lived eight hundred miles away in her hometown of Sleepy Hollow, New York—when he made the stealth purchase. She couldn't even comprehend what type of store would vend such monstrously over-the-top decorations—though, in retrospect, she imagined it was less a baby or home improvement store than it was an agent of a sinister dark force that had made the sale. But when she arrived home from the unbearable festivities, laden down with a host of presents she had not requested and a rash of germs garnered from far too many overly comfortable touches and cheek kisses, well, there it was, waiting for her, in a pile in the center of the guestroom-cum-nursery.

The clown, of course, was on top.

Its visage startled her, and Lana let out a shriek, dropping the bags of bottle sanitizers and too-cute onesies to the polished wooden floor. She was startled by the sight, of course, and on edge from the incessant questions from Granny Lily and the spinster aunts about the baby's name, when she/he would have a sibling, and just what the babysitting rotation would be when Lana returned to her teaching job after Thanksgiving. But she was even more shocked by the image of the clown itself.

To her eyes, it was the most hideous sight she had ever seen.

It would, of course, haunt her in a far more horrific fashion in the weeks to come, but for now, the disgust crept into the space between her vertebrae and clenched down on her spine.

It was hard for her, upon reflection, to pin down exactly what it was about the two-dimensional design of the stick-on that chilled her to her core. Perhaps it was the sloppy, off-color makeup design on its face: a crooked magenta smile, too large for the narrow, wrinkled face, or the teal eye accents that haloed squinty, crow-footed eyes.

Or maybe it was the jagged tufts of pea-green hair that burst forth at an aggressive angle. Or it could have been the clown's clothing, a patchwork of plaid and polka dot, horizontal and vertical stripes, arranged in a simultaneously hypnotic and jarring tableau that covered the length of its lean, shapeless form.

In short, the clown was a black hole of hideous design, but it should have been little more than that. Lana could not comprehend, then, why the sight of it rattled her so.

But she shook off the creeping feeling of dread, and dove into the pile to see what lay underneath the hideous creature.

Though she was already fragile from hormones and lack of sleep, the rest of the offending heap of tasteless decorations was, well, if not harmless, than at least not bone-chilling.

She examined the other figures: the lion tamers and bears balancing on balls, and rings and top hats and miscellany, as well as the gallons of hideous, radioactive paint.

As she did so, Max entered the room, apparently drawn, slowly but surely, by his wife's scream. He let out a small chortle at seeing Lana's obvious discomfort, and after absorbing her withering look, wished her luck in decorating the room with his chosen accouterments.

That sort of behavior—utter disdain for her choices and unrealistic demands on her time and energy—would have shocked and sickened her, if it had not been so typical of their relationship.

She sighed in acceptance, spread out the drop cloth, and after turning the clown face down to avoid its wicked gaze, she started painting the room.

The gaudy nursery would have been little more than an annoyance to Lana, had it not been for the visions.

They didn't start, though, until after the birth of her child. Carla Lilly Mitchell did not come into the world willingly. She had stayed in breech position, stubbornly refusing to turn over, no matter what her mother tried, from a painful version procedure to placing a bag of frozen peas on her belly to try and get the little gal to spin around on her own.

That, plus Lana's chronic high blood pressure, ostensibly caused by medical reasons, led the doctors to declare that Carla would enter the world in the same fashion as Julius Caesar himself.

It was only two days after Mom and baby returned from the hospital—the same day Max returned to his government job pushing government papers across a government desk and earning copious piles of government cash that he spent on thoughtful items, like terrifying nursery decorations—that the terror started.

It all began with a laugh.

The past forty-eight hours, since the two girls had returned from their stay in the hospital, cleared by doctors and blessed by the overly ebullient nurses, had been filled with cries—and screams and wails. These were not the shouts of fear—those would come soon enough—but rather the typical cries of a preemie adjusting to life outside the womb.

It was not, apparently, an easy transition.

Little Carla, for her diminutive size, certainly did have lung power, Lana had to admit, and did she ever use it.

In the various classes the mom-to-be had taken, Lana had been assured that a newborn would sleep twelve, fourteen or, some joked, twenty-eight hours a day. Carla, though, had apparently not received that memo.

The stubborn little girl refused to nap and was picky about the breast as well. She seemed content, it seemed, to cry and shout and fuss about for hours on end.

All of this behavior had the effect of fraying poor Lana's already fragile nerves. Her life, it seemed, consisted of little more than struggling to get her daughter to take the breast, fretting about why she was crying, and desperately attempting to steal a few moments of sleep in between. There was no room in her life for other things, like showering or cleaning up after herself, and God forbid that Max should take on any of those duties. Why, it would severely cut into his television viewing time.

So it was, on the first day of The Terror—as she would later think of it—that Lana found herself attempting to decipher the bizarre contraption known as a 'breast pump.' It was frustrating to say the least, especially for a woman whose thoughts were fogged with clouds of fatigue and lingering thoughts of disappointment in herself and her motherly instincts.

It was one of the rare instances where Carla had deemed it appropriate to take an afternoon nap. Eschewing a nap of her own, Lana had scurried to the kitchen with the baby monitor in tow. Through the static-filled speaker, Lana could hear Carla fussing around in her bassinet, a low steady breathing alternating with small, choking sobs.

It was simultaneously soothing to the new mother—the sounds indicated that her newborn was indeed, still alive and kicking. A fear of SIDS was merely one item on the enormous list of phobias that life had saddled Lana with, but it also irked her, as she was unable to communicate to the wordless child the importance of sleep, for mother and daughter alike.

Just as the frustration rose in her spine, trickling into fingers that fumbled with tubes and cones, something on the monitor…changed.

"Heh, heh, hee."

At first, Lana thought it was a trick of the static so she kept working.

"Heh-heh, hee-hee."

The second time she heard the noise, she paused, setting down the frustrating paraphernalia and looking askance at the receiver.

But as she stared at it, all she could hear was the breathing and gurgling of her daughter.

Lana shook her head. She wished she had shelled out the extra money for the deluxe monitor, the one with the high-definition video and ultra-clear audio. At least that's what it said in the advertisements. But her frugal nature had kicked in, and she'd opted for the temptingly on-sale device.

But now, apparently, it was acting up.

She stared at the faulty device for a few more seconds, willing it to make more unusual noises, but stubbornly, it did no such thing.

She frowned in annoyance, and considered adjusting the dials, wondering if a change of channel or frequency would clear up the static issue, but the device itself seemed obstinately unreceptive to change. Apparently, this could only be done at the base station, so Lana was left contemplating a stealthy trip into the nursery.

That of course, was a recipe for a meltdown. Carla, it seemed, had inherited preternatural senses from some apparently superheroic ancestor with recessive genes that lured in the roots of Lana's family tree.

Lana shook her head. Of course she would not breach the threshold of the nursery for such a silly reason. After all, the noise was likely just a trick of the electronics.

"Caaarrrrllaaaa. Hee-hee-hee-heeeeee."

That could be no burst of static. Lana had heard her daughter's name through the baby monitor. There was no mistaking it. Someone had *said* Carla's name. Someone was in the nursery.

She bolted from her seat in the kitchen, stumbling across the living room, wincing as her strained, recently-recovered-from-surgery body cried out in discomfort.

She tripped on an empty diaper bag—denim and hideous, a gift from her sister-in-law—and spilled the breast pump equipment, still clutched in her hands, against the closed door of the nursery.

"Waahhhhhhhh!"

Lana swore under her breath, hoping that her newborn would not hear the horrid curses and subliminally absorb them, leading to a lifetime of sailor-like vocabulary, and flung open the door, her eyes sweeping across all corners of the room, to find…

That there was no one there.

Of *course* there was no one there. She could have kicked herself. There was no way that a kidnapper or child murderer could have snuck into the house without her knowledge. The doors were locked, as were the windows.

At least, she thought the windows were locked.

She bolted past Carla, who was screaming at the top of her lungs, awoken from her fitful sleep by the banging open of the nursery door.

Lana ignored her baby. She ran to the window and pulled on the sash.

It was locked.

With an enormous exhalation of breath, she dropped to the polished wooden floor of the nursery, huddled with arms around her knees next to the balloon-themed nightlight that cast its soft glow on the circus festivities.

Then her eyes fell on the clown.

She did a double take, an actual, comical whipping of her head, like an actor would do in a movie. But it was no gag. It was a pure, unadulterated reaction of shock and horror.

The clown was…different.

She had placed it on the wall herself, had stuck up its hideous countenance on the screeching orange wall with a quiver in her stomach.

Lana had placed the clown in the only spot she could stand. It was as far away from her daughter's bassinet as possible. Even still, it dominated the northern wall of the nursery, with its sinister grin and cacophonous color scheme. It had stood, its arms and legs akimbo, in some sort of twisted vigil over the baby for the past two days, since Carla had arrived home.

But now…

Now, its positioning had changed. Instead of leaping in the air, as if caught in mid-jumping jack, the clown now seemed to be standing, though bent at the waist, as if hunched over. As if hunched over a baby's crib.

Lana leapt to her feet, the motion startling the already upset baby even further. She strode across the nursery with a mixture of speed and dread, standing on her tiptoes to take a closer look at the clown's face.

Its mouth was open.

Lana knew when she had placed it on the wall, that the figure's mouth had been closed in a tight line, the smear of color serving as an exaggerated smile in place of actual mirth. But now the clown's face featured a gaping maw, and two rows of yellowed, crooked and pointed teeth, framed an oily black tongue.

The mouth looked almost as if it was caught in mid-speech.

As she stared at the stick-on clown, Lana could feel her hand reaching up to touch it, seeking to ascertain through tactile sensation if it was indeed real, or a merely a figure of her fatigued imagination.

But then Carla shrieked again, and Lana's mothering instincts kicked in. She spun unevenly on her heel and headed over to her daughter.

She hefted the tiny baby from her bed and pulled her close.

"There, there," she said in a voice that was intended to be soothing, but came out instead, as a quavering mass of discordant syllables.

"Everything will be okay. Mommy's here."

The words and the touch did not serve to calm the crying baby, and Lana began to feel a wave of panic welling up in her gut. She was unable to comfort her child. She had failed as a mother, and on top of all of that, her imagination was clearly running wild.

She wanted to scream, but as she opened her mouth, she then caught a whiff of the real reason Carla was crying.

So, she took a few moments, changed the baby's soiled diaper, and soothed Carla to sleep in her glider rocker.

After some deliberation, Lana decided not to mention the events of the afternoon to Max when he arrived home. Instead, she fed him the dinner she had hastily prepared—steamed chicken breast and broccoli. Max was a lot of things, but a picky eater perhaps most of all.

She dutifully asked him about his day.

He spoke at great length about paperwork of some sort—filling it out, then filling it out again when some co-worker made a mistake on their end, causing no end of frustration for poor Max who'd never suffered fools gladly—and other matters of grand importance. She listened as best she could, as fatigue tugged at her brain and dragged her eyelids toward the nearly full plate in front of her.

Max gave some perfunctory attention to his only child, awkwardly holding Carla as she screamed, then making timid excuses to avoid changing her, such as suddenly remembering an urgent work call he had to take in his office when it came time for Lana to breastfeed Carla.

A few hours later, with Max passed out on the couch, the clichéd empty beer cans strewn across the living room carpet, Lana was finally able to get Carla down for her bedtime.

Normally, that accomplishment filled Lana with, if not a sense of fulfillment in her motherly duties, a small sense of relief from the incessant demands of a life form completely dependent on her.

At this point, part of her wanted to take a few moments to herself. She longed to get on her computer and trade missives with her best friend who lived eight hundred miles away, or to take a few moments to read a page or two of her favorite book. But the bone-draining fatigue was dragging her to bed, even if a gnawing sense of dread and doubt had taken root in the back of her mind, urging her toward panic and paranoia.

This was a result, of course, of her nighttime ritual of placing the receiver of the baby monitor by the side of her bed. There was no thought given to the idea that Max would place the monitor by his bed, which was located on the second floor, an entire flight away from Lana and Carla, so he could get some sleep.

She hesitated to switch it on, her memories flooding back to the events of that afternoon. The grating screech of electronic laughter rattled around in her brain and the awful sight of that open-mouthed clown was painted on the inside of her eyelids. Lana knew she was just overreacting to stimuli that likely didn't exist, but her thumping heart would not let it go.

It was for this reason that, despite her extreme fatigue, she found herself staring at the monitor for what seemed like hours.

But to her relief, nothing out of the ordinary happened.

The ordinary, though, had taken hold during her vigil. Lana's poor, overworked bladder was crying out for relief.

It was at times like these when she wished she'd taken the master bedroom upstairs. It did, after all, have an attached bathroom. But Max had insisted that she move downstairs when she got pregnant, and truth be told, she appreciated the proximity to her baby.

As she padded past the nursery on the way to the bathroom, Lana paused for a moment. Carla was in a rare state of deep slumber, and Lana wanted nothing more than to gaze at the sleeping beauty. But twin fears—of waking the baby, and of course, seeing the horrific image of the clown—gave her pause.

Perhaps on the way back from the toilet, she mused.

Lana waddled into the bathroom, and by the glow of the small nightlight, did her business. Then she dragged herself to the sink, where she washed her hands and splashed cold water on her face. As she appreciated the sensation of the cold water on her pores, her ears perked up involuntarily.

Was that a creak?

She turned off the water and craned her head toward the hallway, as if that few inches of movement or angular momentum would help the clarity of the noise.

Nothing.

She walked over and opened the door, peering into the darkness of the hallway. Once again, she saw nothing, even as she waited for her eyes to adjust. She turned back to the bathroom, ready to scrub a face that had not been sufficiently cleaned in ages.

As Lana bent down to turn the faucet back on once more, she heard another noise.

Creak, squeak.

She froze. She knew the floorboards in the downstairs hall were prone to creaking under footsteps, but a squeak?

Squeak, creak, squeak.

Her mind, unbidden, flew to the image of the clown, and its horrid multicolored jumpsuit and its large, cartoonish purple shoes.

What squeaked? Clown shoes squeaked.

Creak, squeak, creak.

Lana closed her eyes and took a deep breath—or tried to. Her breath instead came in small, rapid bursts, as the anxiety she had fought with all her life crept up inside her chest.

She gripped the cold tile of the sink until her fingers ached, and held her breath.

Nothing.

She counted to ten, stumbling on the pesky middle numbers a bit, starting over, and finally coming close enough. She exhaled her captive breath in a rush.

She opened her eyes.

And screamed.

There, in the mirror before her, she saw it.

The horrid, cacophonous visage of the clown, its mouth wide open in mid-cackle or pre-bite, its floppy arms and claw-like fingers spread wide, ready to envelop her in a smothering embrace.

She shrieked and dropped to her knees, pain shooting through her kneecaps as they collided with the cold tiles on the bathroom floor.

Her heart slammed against her ribcage, and her lungs refused to draw breath. She raised her arm to protect her face, ready for the inevitable.

After a beat, she opened her eyes.

There, above her, was nothing.

She stood slowly, flipping on the light and examining every corner of the bathroom. No one was there. Nothing was threatening her.

She took a deep breath, and hugging herself tight, she returned to her bed, where a dreamless sleep overtook her, until the cries of her daughter woke her in the pre-dawn hours.

Lana had, over the past few days, lost all sense of morning, noon and night. The only clock that held sway over her day was the incessant need to feed her preemie, in a desperate attempt to get Carla's weight up to an acceptable level.

Upon her first cries, Lana had sprung from her bed, scooped the baby from the bassinet without even a glance around the room, and took her into the den, where Carla lazily sucked on Mama's teat and Lana numbed her mind watching infomercials. She lost herself in a fog of miracle cutlery and wild topless college girls, until Max stumbled across her field of view, rushing out the front door, late as usual for his ever-important government job.

If the ceaseless fog of fatigue had any benefit for Lana, it was that the weight of her sleep deficit made it nearly impossible for her to fixate on the odd events of the day before.

Nearly, of course, was not the same as entirely.

Though she would not admit it, Lana did, in fact, have many talents. She had been, in her youth, a fine actress, nearly snagging roles as the plucky best friend in two different network sitcoms and actually scoring a small role in a comedic film directed by an up-and-coming star. But she had backed out of the project upon learning she would need to show her bare breasts on film.

She was also quite a writer, with a sharp, observant voice. But her creative endeavors had inevitably been subsumed by other aspects of her life. Teaching spoiled sixth graders, tending to her fine suburban home and upstanding husband, and partaking in worthwhile pastimes by the side of her Junior League companions had given her little time to pursue anything artistic.

But that didn't mean Lana's imagination had lain fallow. She had spent many nights, alone in her queen-sized bed except for the baby gestating in her womb, imagining stories in her mind. They were not science fiction epics, as had been her passion as a teen-ager. Nor were they tales of erotica, which she and her friend had crafted in their spare time, unleashing their pent-up sexuality on the page to the tune of torrid encounters replete with details that would make her southern mother-in-law blush.

Now, though, her imagination was slave to dark thoughts. She had imagined, in the past eight months or so, every possible disastrous outcome that could possibly come to pass, from another tragic miscarriage, to dropping her newborn on the pavement of the hospital on the way home.

She had never, though, allowed her mind to wander into the fantastical realm in which it apparently now resided. There was no logical way, of course, that an evil clown could be stalking her in her own home, that a cursed wall adhesive could come to life and threaten her and Carla.

Or could there?

She shook her head with vigor, as if she could dislodge the crazy thoughts from her mind with the sheer force of will coupled with momentum. After a few seconds of this, she glanced down to see Carla, squinting up with a quizzical look on her face.

Lana smiled for the first time in ages, then, and released her anxiety with a guttural laugh.

To say Lana spent the day in a normal fashion would be mis-leading. She kept every light in her home on, and kept off every source of noise in the off position: television, radio, computer and cell phone. She also dragged Carla's bassinet into the den and kept the door to the nursery closed.

Even if she was sure it was all in her imagination, she was not going to take any chances with her own peace of mind.

It was, therefore, a rather uneventful day.

This time, at least, Max had called.

He was working late, he said. It was not an uncommon circumstance, though early on in their marriage Lana would wait up and fret for him, sending out occasional text messages inquiring to his whereabouts.

When he would come home, often quite late, he would berate her for pestering him, and explain in a condescending voice that his job was quite important and that he frequently had to work late.

If he had not been such an asexual creature, Lana might have imagined that he was having an affair. In fact, there had been a time in her life when she had wished that he would take a lover—male or female—so that she would have a reason to leave him and pursue other avenues. But now, with Carla in the picture, Lana knew she would be with him until death do them part, as they said.

His news meant that the meal she had prepared, chicken tacos from a kit—it was the best she could muster—would sit untouched in the refrigerator.

She considered, for a moment, opening one of the bottles of wine she and Max had received from their neighbors, an insufferably cute couple with enough fertility to repopulate the entire state in the event of the zombie apocalypse, but then thought against it. She would not be able to pump and dump her breast milk at this point.

Carla had been better than normal during the day, actually napping and eating more than ever, which Lana took to be a good sign. The oddness and terror of the previous day had nearly faded when it came time to try and put her down for the night.

Thinking herself silly, Lana opted to put the bassinet back in the nursery to put Carla to bed where she belonged.

With the light on in the nursery, Lana took a moment to gaze at the clown. It was as she remembered it: arms and legs akimbo, mouth closed.

She mentally chided herself for letting her imagination run wild, and once Carla was settled in, the light off and monitor on, Lana decided to reward herself with a bit of dessert.

She realized she was out of Hershey's Kisses—she had been snacking on them more than she realized, apparently, or Max had pilfered some of her stash—so she decided to dive into one of the apple pies her mother-in-law had sent over for no discernable reason.

She placed the monitor receiver on the counter and rooted around in the kitchen drawer for her cake server. Not finding it, she decided to improvise, grabbing a carving knife and slicing herself an enormous portion.

As she sat down to eat, though, the monitor crackled.

She put down her fork and stared at it, her heart fluttering in her chest.

Caarrrlllaaaa. Heeehehhheheeeheee.

Lana stood up and took a step toward the monitor, sweat pouring off her brow.

"Hehehehehehee."

"Waaaaaahhhhhhhh!"

Rational thought flew from her mind, and motherly instinct kicked in. She snatched up the carving knife, and ignoring the advice of parents everywhere, she ran with it toward the nursery.

The door was ajar, a faint light pouring through the crack. But she had closed it, hadn't she? She *always* closed it.

The cries from within were mixed with squeaks and creaks, and Lana wanted to scream herself. Instead, she kicked in the door, as if she were a hero in an action movie, rather than a terrified new mother.

Lying on the floor of the nursery was Carla. She was on a blanket and screaming her head off.

Lana's head whipped up, and then she saw it.

The clown had detached from the wall. There it was, in three dimensions, standing over her child, its bony fingers reaching down toward the helpless baby, a string of spittle dripping from its pointed teeth.

Lana let out a blood-curdling scream and leapt toward the clown, waving the knife in a wide arc. She stumbled as she went, tripping over some cheap, plastic wheeled toy that was several months away from being interesting to the newborn.

As she spun through the air, Lana tried to keep herself from falling on top of the helpless, screaming baby, and as she fell, she spun her body around, ready to defend her child from the horrible monstrosity that threatened her.

Lana landed in a heap on the hardwood floor, a jolt of pain shooting up her back, stars dancing in front of her eyes.

She let out a primal scream and lashed out with the knife, striking not paper-thin adhesive, but solid flesh.

Crying out in triumph, she slashed and stabbed again and again, over and over, unleashing the frustration and anger that had been bottled up inside her.

Then, when she had expended all the energy within her, she opened her eyes… and did not shed a tear over the shredded body of Max, sprawled out on the floor, his lifeblood spreading across the hardwood, seeping into the baby blanket and welling up, red against the shocking orange of the nursery wall.

THE GREAT PIE FIGHT

JOHN SKERCHOCK

"Change is constant and inevitable. It is always around us. It is subtle like the flap of a butterfly's wings. Yet when it happens we are caught by surprise. Change cannot be stopped. Even a stagnant pond is constantly changing, creating and revealing miracles only to surpass them with other miracles. Change begets change."
—Albus Mendocci, alchemist 1356-15?

My name is Giz. You don't know me. No one knows me. I am one of the imps, tasked with doing the daily duties of helping run the infernal empire created by My Lord, Satan. It is He that I serve as I was one of the cherubs who took his side during the Great War before the birth of man. I curse and adore Him.

I am tasked with telling you the story of a most evil person. He is the most evil of all who have wandered the aimless halls of Hell. It is only a creature of the most evil kind who could do what he did and survive the wrath of my Master. He was a fucking clown.

It was Mime Day. Every day was Mime Day. Yesterday was Mime Day. Tomorrow will be Mime Day. The day after tomorrow will be Mime Day. The day never changed. The routine never changed. That's the way it was in Hell.

Beepo the clown picked up a cream pie from the counter and threw it at the mime across the room in the invisible box. It was a real invisible box and not the imaginary ones that mimes pretended to be trapped in. This mime was trapped for all eternity in an invisible box he could not escape, but for some reason known only to the Infernal One, cream pies could pass through.

Whop was the sound the pie made as it struck the mime squarely in the face and knocked him backwards. As the mime recovered, Beepo picked up another pie and threw it at him. *Whop!* Another direct hit and the mime staggered backwards.

Being in Hell was doing the same thing over and over and over again. It was boredom squared. It was eternal agony of the mind. The suffering was intense and, honestly, quite boring. There was no meaning; no purpose to the task Beepo was performing. It was his sentence, and he was miserable.

The torment and mental anguish Beepo suffered was compounded by the fact that his sin was replayed constantly in his brain. Beepo had been a clown in a nameless circus sometime in the past. It may have been yesterday, last week, last year. He didn't know. Time was difficult to understand in Hell. There was no hope, only despair.

As Beepo picked up another pie and threw it, in his mind he relived his last minutes on earth, but instead of suffering because of it, he was wondering how a practical joke could send him here.

Beepo was one of eight clowns stuffed into a tiny automobile about to make their big appearance in the center ring. Beepo wore blackface and it was his job to get out of the car last and sing *Mammy* as the empty car chugged out of sight.

The car was entering the ring when Beepo got the urge to fart. He'd eaten a big lunch of greasy sausage and fries and needed to let one rip. It would be loud and it would be stinky, and the other clowns would bitch and moan later, but Beepo knew this fart was something special.

Without a second thought, and an action that sealed his fate, he whipped out his Zippo and lit the flame. He held it between his legs as he arched back to let the largest, gaseous fart in his life escape from his butt. The burst of gas would make a big blue flash as the methane hit the flame. It would happen just as the car came to a stop. It would astound the audience.

It did more than that because Beepo didn't know that the car had a gas leak of its own. As the methane from the fart hit the small flame, the resulting blue blast of fire ignited the leaking gas. The explosion sent bits of clown and car parts flying high into the sky and the audience, to then catch the people and tent on fire. It would have been hilarious if not for the death and injury it had caused.

Well, Beepo still got a chuckle out of it even though he wasn't supposed to. In a very dark way it was funny, but it was an accident. Why did he have to go to Hell for it?

Beepo picked up another pie and threw it at the mime.

No demons poked him with pitch forks. No demons taunted him or cajoled him. The overseers of that division were half asleep as they went about their rounds in a stupor. Even they were bored from the never-ending monotony. It was just him and the mime, and Beepo could look to his left and to his right and see other clowns in other rooms—all of the rooms had clear glass walls— picking up pies and throwing them at mimes. All of them were suffering their own personal hells of boredom and monotony.

What the other clowns did to be here, Beepo didn't know. Nor did he know what act forced the mimes to suffer through eternity, although the fact that they were mimes probably spoke for itself. Perhaps it was true that nobody liked a mime, even the Holy Father.

But then something happened. In the grand scheme of things it could hardly be noticed. The demons were no longer as watchful as they once were so no one but Beepo and his mime saw it. To this day no one knows how it happened because it couldn't happen. It shouldn't have happened, but, somehow, it did.

An act of free will had somehow managed to enter the bowels of Hell!

After throwing pie after pie after pie millions of times over to the same mime that took the hit and staggered backwards only to recover and get hit again, Beepo missed! Perhaps he was too deep in thought? We'll never know. The only thing certain is that he missed.

It may have gotten a little colder in Hell because suddenly the mime gave him the finger.

Beepo blinked and grabbed a pie. Something was happening. Something was raging inside of him. He felt lighter, as if chains were falling from his sides. Fog was lifting from his brain and an emotion was seeping in.

The mime was taunting him, and Beepo felt angry. He picked up another pie. He threw it hard and missed again! The mime fell backward, holding his stomach and pretending to laugh hysterically.

What was going on?

Somewhere in the great underworld known as Hell, Satan sat on his infernal throne, despondent. He had taken a crap on Hitler earlier that morning and it brought him no joy. The mad dictator simply took it and walked away; there was no plea for mercy.

Satan was leaning over an arm of his throne with chin in hand, wondering how He could have been so stupid. He had been taken by the Creator of All Things. He, the Lord of Lies, the Master of Deceit, had Himself been deceived when the Lord had reached out to Him.

God, so kind and loving, had become disillusioned. He was tired of being so forgiving. It was frustrating Him. People committed sins willingly, knowingly. Mafia dons would kill people, feed drugs to children, and then ask forgiveness in church in order to get into Heaven. People would cheat on their spouses, ask forgiveness, and then do it again. It had all become so hypocritical, and God had become weary of it all.

So He reached out. He reached out to Lucifer, once His favorite, and offered a deal. For centuries they had struggled, and God still wanting to be a kind God, allowed Satan to make his trips to Earth to try to sway a soul or two in his favor. Now God was offering Him more than He could ever want. No longer would He be stuck with just despots, child molesters, animal abusers, and scientologists. He could have more, much more.

His Infernal Majesty was so overcome with the deal that He forgot to stop and think there may be a catch. Often, if a deal is too good, something's wrong. This wasn't the first time Satan was so tricked. It had happened before.

Years ago, Satan had pleaded with the Creator of All Things to let Him have music in His infernal realm. Demons playing instruments just didn't cut it, and He was getting tired of playing the fiddle.

God had showed compassion.

Satan licked His lips as He thought of all of those rock musicians who used drugs and cheated on their wives. He was certain they would be allowed within His fold. Yet God had tricked Him—God only allowed him disco music.

The walls of Hell shook that day as Satan's rage was felt in every crack and crevice within the ancient halls. Demons and souls suffered alike from his wrath, and the constant disco tunes that had followed.

As the disco ball twirled above Satan's throne, His Infernal Majesty sat despondent over being tricked again.

God had been true to His word. The souls came en masse. There were more than He could count; more than He had room for at first. Hell grew by leaps and bounds and soon the demons were over worked. It was they, not the souls, who were being punished.

They came in groups of a hundred or more too fast to be processed, and they were already mind-numbed from the boring lives they had led. It was too much. Satan's time was devoted only to Hell. He could no longer take the luxury of a trip to Earth to lure a soul to his realm. He now spent more time trying to figure out how to get them all out! Oh, to have the peacefulness of a few moans and blood curdling screams again!

It was nuts! The sadists were punished by being tortured by the masochists. The masochists began to enjoy their job inflicting pain, and the sadists began to become masochists as they learned to enjoy the pain. The despots no longer minded being crapped upon by Satan. The child molesters were used to having their weenies hacked off and were becoming masochists or sadists and that just messed up all the data.

Satan just sat and sighed while The Hustle played in the background. He just shook His head. At least He would be getting that twerking bitch in a few years. She sealed her fate smoking pot on stage, but unfortunately, her shit wasn't much better than disco.

It was Azal, one of the Greater Demons, who brought Satan out of his doldrums by bringing him news.

"My Infernal Lord, there's something funny going on in sector seven-dash-eighty-dash-three, Sire."

Satan rolled His eyes. "That's the clown section. Of course something funny is going on down there."

"Uh, no, My Lord. I mean odd or strange. Not funny ha-ha."

Satan dismissed the demon with a wave of His hand.

Beepo had an urge, and it felt strange at first. His brain had been so numbed from the onerous routine of throwing pie after pie that it took him by surprise.

Suddenly, he was on his right knee with his hands at his heart, belting out the words to Mammy. He sang them as he had never sung them before; he was loud and confident. The other clowns and mimes began to look at him. Many stared uncomprehending; a few shrunk back out of fear, but the rest began to laugh and join in.

As they reached the final line, the crescendo was deafening, and when Beepo hit the last word, "Mammy!" he dragged it out so loud and vibrant that he shattered all of the glass walls in the entire clown division. It was amazing.

Clowns began to hoot and holler and laugh hysterically. The mimes began to look around in wonder.

Suddenly, an idea blinked into the head of one of the mimes. After enduring millions upon millions of pies in the face, he ran forward and grabbed a pie off the table and threw it into the face of another clown.

Another mime did the same. Soon, all hell broke loose in Hell as clowns and mimes pelted each other with pies. Lesser demons and imps awoke from their robotic slumber to find themselves being pelted with the creamy pastries. Some blinked and just went back to sleep. Others joined in and began pelting clowns, mimes, and other demons and imps with cream pies.

The fracas boiled over into other divisions as an endless army of souls was pelted. The narcissists were the favorite target of the sadists, as they bitched and moaned that the pies would ruin their good looks. The masochists wouldn't throw pies but begged and pleaded to have pies thrown at them.

Beepo was throwing pies, dodging pies thrown at him, and laughing like he had never laughed before. Who could have thought that someone could actually have a good time in Hell?

Satan met daily with his hierarchy in their board room. Although it may as well have been called a *bored* room for how lively everyone was. His personnel were exhausted trying to maintain records, mete out punishments, deter hope, and many thousands of other details designed to torment souls throughout eternity.

Satan only meant to have a brief meeting, then go to lunch at Dante's Infernal Deli. He felt like gnawing on the bones of some non-believers, but then even that was getting boring.

It was Baal who brought up the disturbance in sector-seven-dash-eight-dash-three. It apparently had spilled over to adjoining sectors. "I think this is serious, My Lord," he finished.

Satan, not yet at His seat, looked across the smoldering table top at the faces of His loyal colleagues, those that had fought with him during the Great Rebellion, and sighed. He then fell back into His chair and let out a wet, flatulent *"FLLLLPHHH!"*

Livicticus burst out laughing and was immediately banished to the top of an iceberg somewhere in the arctic with a mere flick of Satan's finger. Satan wasn't pleased. The Infernal Master stood up and looked at the chair. Some damned infernal dog had placed a whoopee cushion there and He had sat squarely upon it.

Other demons smirked and tittered but none were as so bold as Livicticus to burst out laughing. It would be months before he was back within the fold. The remaining demons struggled with themselves to pretend not to have noticed the incident.

"Let's find out what's going on, and then we go to lunch!" the Dark Lord said as He rose from the accursed chair. "I will make the one responsible for this outrage suffer My eternal fury!"

Satan and His staff proceeded to the elevator and took it down to sector seven-dash-eighty-dash-three. Aside from the horns protruding from their foreheads, they looked just like business-men going to a meeting. In fact, Pazuzu suggested they do exactly that after they checked on the disturbance, but the rest wanted to go to lunch.

When the elevator doors opened, Pazuzu began to step out and was immediately struck by a pie in the face. Satan let out a chuckle and pushed the half-asleep demon guard out of His way as Satan studied the chaos going on around Him.

Pies were flying fast and furious. They splattered everywhere. Some whipped cream got onto Satan's sleeve and Azal tried to wipe it off. That's when a pie struck Satan on the side of the face. The foil pie pan stuck to one of His horns, and Pazuzu began to laugh at Satan as he struggled to get it off his master.

His Infernal Majesty pushed the demon aside and in a loud, commanding voice declared, "What is going on in here?" Satan's eyes were piercing as He searched through the voluminous crowd of demons and souls. Finally, they settled on Beepo.

Half of the clown's blackface was gone, wiped away by a number of pie hits to the face.

Other clowns and mimes backed away, leaving Beepo standing alone.

His Infernal Majesty grew three times His size that day, bursting out of His suit and shoes as His full figure evolved: that of the cloven-hoofed, bare-chested, horned-deity of old.

In four short steps He was standing before the rebellious clown. With His hands on His hips, Satan, never looking more majestic or more menacing, looked down upon the slight frame of the diminutive clown. He bellowed, "What kind of puny soul dares to disturb my realm?"

The voice was loud and frightening. Even the greater demons trembled a bit when they heard it, but not Beepo.

Defiant, the clown stood before His Infernal Majesty and yelled right back at Him, "I don't deserve to be here. It was just a fart, for Christ's sake!"

The imps and demons howled at hearing the Almighty's name mentioned in the bowels of Hell. Even the greater demons felt fear.

"How dare you make a mockery of your infernal punishment! I shall sentence you for all eternity to…uh…to…" But the Grand, Infernal Master couldn't think of a punishment. He was stumped. Years of boredom had taken their toll, and as He stood before His minions and millions of tormented souls, He could not think of a thing to say.

That was when another pie hit Him in the face. No one saw who threw it, but many were convinced it was Beepo because he stood the closest. Satan was so taken aback that He actually stumbled backwards, crushing two minor demons in His way.

No one knew what to do. An affront of this caliber to His Infernal Majesty had never before happened in the history of Hell. Satan just stood there, blinking in disbelief. The silence was deafening!

Then the mime laughed.

It was a deep, gut-busting, hearty laugh that broke the silence of Hell…and it came from a mime!

Suddenly, everyone was laughing and Satan just stood there, in His Infernal glory, covered with cream pie all over His face.

And just like that He was gone. Satan simply said, "Fuck it," and vanished in a puff of sulfur-laden smoke.

The greater demons were left scratching their heads as they were pelted with pies. Beepo was cheered and promoted up the ladder to Infernal Majesty pro tem.

It all changed that day.

An ounce of free will had let hope in through the gates of Hell and chased the Devil out.

I sat through this, avoiding pies and laughing mimes, to make note of this strange turn of events.

I fear Beepo.

He is most evil and diabolical soul I have ever seen. I long for the return of my Master who now wanders through Purgatory looking for a purpose.

It's not the same anymore.

It never is.

WHAT HAPPENS WHEN YOU DON'T BELIEVE IN HALLOWEEN

GARY WEDLUND

Little Johnny Bo kicked me in the shin and it bled. When it happened, I was talking to his mother, my sister, Ellen. At first I thought she hadn't noticed, but he did it again, and she kept right on chatting about the clown festival. Apparently, assault and battery on recently divorced Uncle Jim from, "Way up north in the city of Ohio," was normal.

I wanted to beat the little fucker blue with a three-inch belt. But *we* didn't believe in corporal punishment, so I'd have settled for a time out in a dog cage. I didn't make mention. We weren't a close family. In fact, I'd just met the brat the day prior, after driving six hundred miles and barging in on chitlins and greens, uninvited.

"And I have just the costume for you," Ellen said, then dragged me into the guest bedroom where I'd dropped my bag the day before when I'd imposed myself upon them. She opened the closet door and pulled out a red dress that I remembered having last seen on Mom, *God rest her soul*. It was the garish red one, with huge white poke dots.

"I'm a guy. I'm not wearing that."

"Oh, shush," she said. "I'll just rip off the white collar, and I can widen the seams on a black pair of pants so they bloom out. Oh, it's going to be crazy good."

"Uh-huh."

"I also got the best boots at the Goodwill. They're size fourteen. They said, 'I didn't think no one would'a ever wanted those ugly ol' things.' God put them there for you, and for just a quarter." She kicked them at me.

I wedged off a shoe and put a foot in without untying the laces. Air whooshed up. The room suddenly smelled like a Brooklyn back-alley stoop.

"I'll spray paint them purple. You can wear extra socks," Ellen said. Then she was gone, carrying the boots, dress and a couple pair of Mom's zip-up-the-side slacks. Mom had been pretty wide, so the thought of doubling the fabric into bloomers seemed over-kill. I heard a rip, then the sewing machine whirling. Ellen was the fastest seamstress in Porkertown, Mississippi. That and laundry were how she made her spending money.

Johnny Bo came in, grinned up at me, kicked my other shin and left. I slammed the door, locked it, found some porn magazines at the bottom of my suitcase and whacked my wiener. I hoped to bleed off the frustration like I heard chimpanzees did almost all the time. I couldn't concentrate. Johnny Bo had planted himself on the other side of the door and was leaning on it while scraping it with something that was likely making marks. The panel bulged in and out from his weight.

Bang, bang, bang. "Are you in there, Jim?" this time the voice was female.

I caught skin pulling up my zipper and opened the door.

Sis tossed in the dress and a Marilyn Monroe wig that she'd frosted Day-Glo green and purple. "Hurry up. We leave for the party in ten minutes."

Johnny Bo stuck his tongue out at me from behind Sis.

"Isn't he cute. Johnny Bo's been so excited to finally meet his uncle," my clueless sister said before closing the door so I could dress in the homemade clown outfit for the party at his school.

I sat in the back seat of the Lincoln with a stiff neck, while my sister pasted white goop on my face. *What kind of idiot buys a Lincoln?* George, her husband, was driving while humming *Amazing Grace* and picking his nose. He was a bodybuilder, which he mentioned a lot, like it was a memoir he could pass on to his kids. Johnny Bo rode shotgun, making finger-gun gestures at passing cars.

"Pucker!"

Lipstick was added. Then she put dots all over my face. The pink bow tied near my belly button was the size of a truck tire.

I was helpless; she'd duck-taped rubber garden gloves on my hands. They were also five sizes too big. I was hungry. No way could I eat the hors d'oeuvres and cake with fingers the size of Polish sausages.

"What do I do?" My size fourteens flopped down the hallway to Johnny Bo's second grade classroom.

"Just wave your arms, laugh and fall down. Bending over and letting the other clowns kick you might also be fun," Sis said.

Johnny Bo laughed, making it the only time during the trip that he paid attention.

Every so often a child walked by and either backed away with orbs for eyes or jumped around, pointing and laughing at me. "They're laughing at me."

"You're a clown, Jim. They're supposed to laugh at you," Ellen said while dragging me forward by my arm.

George had stayed outside. He was chumming it up with the other men, drinking Dr. Pepper out of an iced cooler and hovering over a BBQ grill. They'd started off with comments about Mississippi Tech before I'd been yanked inside and lost contact. *Fuck Mississippi Tech. Nobody on the whole planet gives a rat's ass about fucking Mississippi Tech.* And what's with Mississippi and Tech—that's oxymoronic. If I'd been left outside with the men, I might have ended up in a fistfight over it with the fathers of *Porkertown Southern Baptist Elementary School.* Getting beat up and arrested seemed better than this.

The teacher clapped her hands with delight on her face as Ellen marched me in to stand next to the other four victims. They'd all rented costumes and didn't look as authentic. All four of them stared straight ahead, too mortified to say hello. Upon closer inspection, one was missing an ear, apparently from a recent accident because the stump seeped. Another sported a bandaged arm. The tall guy staggered a moment, but recovered. The stubby pumpkin-faced guy with the wild black hair needed to change his bloody sock.

No doubt everyone had coerced their deadbeat uncles and aunts into doing the dirty work of playing clown so the hubbies wouldn't miss the BBQ.

I decided to gawk at the classroom décor in order to avoid being grossed out by my disheveled cohorts. Crayoned turkeys lined the blackboard sill. On the other wall were finger paintings, several of stick-finger cowboys shooting Indians. They had one of those big round analogue clocks. The teacher and half a dozen parents were making comments about our contribution as the hands ticked closer to twelve thirty. My stomach grumbled. The kids squirmed in their seats like they all needed to go to the bathroom at the same time. One confirmed it, holding up two fingers.

I felt an obligation to say something, so in a strong voice I asked, "Isn't this Halloween?"

"We don't believe in Halloween," a parent said. She wore a long dress and a bun.

The teacher embellished, "Satan is real, and he manifests himself in a number of ways."

My own sister, Ellen, joined the celebration of stupidity. "That's why we're doing a clown party."

"Well, of course," I said, to shut them up. I wanted to ask if Satan could manifest himself in NASCAR or Merle Haggard, but steered clear for my sister's sake. After all, I needed a temporary place to stay.

Around that time I felt the earth tremble. One of the panes of glass even bulged a little, but nobody else seemed to notice, maybe because earthquakes were rare in Mississippi and they'd never felt one. Everyone was so excited about the festival, too.

A few minutes later an administrator walked in. She put up her hands, calling for quiet. "I have an announcement," she said. "It appears that a gas tank has exploded across town. No need to worry or interrupt our festival." She smiled.

The kids liked that and had a mini-riot.

They marched us into the gym after they settled down. The gym had one of those garage-type doors that emptied into the yard. This had allowed them to set up partitions and some tents just beyond the swing sets, creating an indoor-outdoor carnival environment.

They had games: Bob the apple; Pin the tail on the donkey. Somebody had gotten industrious and made a dunking machine, too. I scooted past that in a hurry and opted for farther outside, where they'd made a crawl-through tunnel, tent to tent. Last was the barrel ride. The barrel ride went down a path between the trees, up along the crest of a wooded hill and down the far edge back to the other side of the festive playground.

A clown in a blue outfit squeaked a bike horn attached to her belt. The outfit looked homemade, which, for some reason, I found appealing after spending some time with my other associates who'd obviously rented and taken the easy way out.

Blue Clown Lady had slightly buck teeth and ran a good fifty pounds overweight. Instead of the gaudy makeup, her face only had a pasted cherry on its nose. I liked her dimples. Her hair was nice, too; brunette, past her shoulders, and not much altered to make her look clownish, other than a few fake flowers here and there.

When I came close, she said, "You're new," which for no rea-son at all informed me she wasn't an idiot. "We're supposed to do this in teams, so they don't get stuck in the woods or go out of control and roll too fast down the last hill."

I took that as a sign and stepped up to the other side of our barrel. "This kind of looks like the haunted trail, which would be… you know… Halloween." The path pretty much disappeared for most of the trip.

"Yeah." She eyed me with care, checking the size of my hands and feet, like that was going to work.

"I'm Jim. I'm living with Ellen because I just got divorced and am a basket case over it. Me and my ex worked at the same place, too. I needed a complete break, but am a bit surprised that I ended up down here in Porkertown."

"Unemployed, then." Disappointment dripped off her lips. Yeah, she wasn't stupid at all.

"Ellen's set me up at the hardware store. I start Monday. It's not much, but it'll do for now. Prices around here appear low. Idle hands are the devil's playthings. Blah, blah, blah and et cetera."

"I'm Janet," she said, "and here come the little fuckers."

I smiled. Then I noticed she was right and lost my grin. They were coming closer, picking barrels. There were ten barrels, manned by twenty clowns. All the other clowns had rented suits and odd pasty faces with dull eyes. I figured it was heredity, and down here that could only mean one thing. It could only mean one, big family thing.

One of the clowns put his barrel on end and knelt inside while his partner pretended to crank a handle. Pop went the weasel. The kids liked that, only God knows why. Those two turned their barrel back on its side and a little redheaded girl crawled in. They started rolling her up the trail. More than likely all the kids would end up so dizzy they'd all puke, but nobody had thought of that.

Five more barrels went by before the first child materialized in front of us. It was Johnny Bo. He went from foot to foot, arms jacking, expecting something. In a minute he was going to kick me.

"Lay over the barrel," Janet said.

I did that.

She kicked me in the ass, making me roll all the way over until the barrel plowed me under.

Johnny Bo loved that, jumping up and down, giggling.

I turned on Janet, but she shoved the barrel and bowled me over. She ran around the thing while making leaping, starfish gestures. When she bent over to help me up, she whispered, "You're doing great." Then she tripped me onto my back again when my guard was down. She rolled the barrel over my corpse-like pose. The sky was blue, up past the willow limbs.

I had to straighten my wig. "Let's just get the brat in the barrel, already," I whispered as she helped me up again.

"You're fun, even if you are clumsy and have tiny hands," she said before helping Johnny Bo crawl into the open end of the barrel.

"Right." I started pushing the rolling barrel into the weeds. Janet helped keep it straight.

Johnny Bo went round and round, laughing so much that I thought he might choke and die. We'd not technically be responsible, given we'd not organized any of this and would have opted for Halloween.

"I work at the hair salon next door to the hardware store," she said.

We rounded a clump of trees. Not a single barrel was in sight in the thick woods, other than our own. My back hurt, and my guess was we'd done about ten percent of the trail. Probably body-builder George had invented the ride.

"I've been divorced three times," she added.

I had to stop for a minute, to catch my breath and figure out why she was relaying her life's history.

"Hey!" Johnny Bo yelled with a barrel echo.

I started pushing him around and around again.

"Well, technically, only a week the first time. I opted for an abortion," she continued. Apparently she'd not heard the term, 'Loose Lips Sink Ships.' "I feel bad about it and have been on birth control ever since. Don't tell anyone about any of that, especially my mother, or I'm in Shitsville. I told them I was on fertility drugs, during my last husband, just to shut them up."

Johnny Bo was laughing so much I might have been mistaken in regards to a word or two of Janet's confessions.

"My lips…are sealed," I panted

"Next time I'm just shacking up," she added.

"That's an unusual…attitude for someone…attending this assembly," I had to say while gasping for air.

"Oh right. You're not from down here, are you? We have more divorces and abortions and sin shacking than any other state in the union. It's just we don't talk about it and mostly blame it on gay conspiracies instead of Elizabeth spreading a Y down at the Piggly Diner. She broke up two of my marriages, and she didn't keep either of the bastards."

Goddamn it. How did that make me like her? She wasn't even much help pushing the barrel. "I've got to meet this Elizabeth." I smirked.

She kicked the barrel extra hard, and I fell on my face.

She laughed, caught up to the barrel and rolled over it, doing clown things with her body.

Johnny Bo stuck his head out the side, pointed and laughed, too.

I sat up, resigned to my fate. "I know slapstick is part of being a clown, but enough already."

She took a step back, staggering a little when the earth shook. The ground rumbled this time. I could hear it from where I sat, but she didn't comment on it.

It might also have been my empty stomach. "Say, how come there aren't any other barrels rolling by?"

Janet shrugged. "Maybe we're going faster than everyone else?"

"Then how come we've not caught anyone?"

"Maybe they're going faster than us?"

"No," I said. "Something's fishy. Maybe we took the wrong path. I'm going to investigate."

"I wanna go around and around and get dizzy," Johnny Bo protested with a head poking out of the barrel's side.

"Just a minute, stay put and hold your horses. I need to investigate."

"I'm going with you." Janet grabbed my rubbery hand.

We walked into the woods, up the rise some, and looked around. There were lots of bushes and trees. Off to the north, I caught sight of a little smoke in the distance, though the leaves made it hard to tell.

"That gas tank probably blew up again," Janet said.

"How does a gas tank blow up again?"

"I just wanted to hear you talk all male and macho while wearing a dress." She winked at me when I turned to study the cherry glued to the tip of her nose. After closing her eyes, she tilted her head up a little and puckered.

How presumptuous, I thought, just before I bent down and ate the cherry off her nose.

"Hey, that has Elmer's on it," she said.

So I kissed her then because her mouth was partially open and she wasn't as aware. "That's what we call spontaneity in the North," I said.

"So, what's it mean in the South?" she asked.

"Probably that they had two gas tanks, side by side. One just took a while to cook." I smiled and led us back down the trail, ignoring the kick to the back of my pants and the squeak of her bicycle horn.

Johnny Bo was pouting. When he saw us he jumped off the barrel and crawled back in. I started pushing him along the wooded crest of the hill, but just before the big drop off, I had to rest again. The trees still hid the view.

People were screaming down below. Obviously, the party was in full swing. God only knew what they had planned to foist upon us clowns next.

"I think we should wait right here for the next barrel to show." Janet sat on the barrel beside me. "That way we can yell at them and call them slackers."

"You just want another kiss."

Janet frowned and sighed.

That made me feel like a cad. "I'm sorry. I sometimes come across as facetious."

She crossed her eyes at my word, but still wouldn't look at me.

"I should have said that I like you," I said. "You're fun. I expected a really awful time here." I smiled at her hazel eyes. "By saying, 'You just want another kiss,' I was really saying I feel at ease with you already and that *I* would like another kiss."

"Really?"

I nodded.

We mugged each others' faces.

* * *

"Hey, it's been forever. Let's go," Johnny Bo screamed, his voice echoing after a while. "I know what you're doing. It's yucky!"

Janet abruptly stood and straightened the bra under her clown shirt.

I walked around like a cowboy and zipped the ridiculous side zipper on my bloomer pants.

Once recovered, I bent and shoved the barrel along the last of the top of the hill. Janet pushed some, too, apparently a little more invigorated. Johnny Bo was happy again, singing the Butthead Song, which I'd never heard before, but it only had one word in the lyrics, so I learned it fast.

We came to the opening prior to the drop down the hill. From there we had a spectacular view of the clown festival and school. Both tents had fallen and lay flat on the ground, though inside, people seemed to be struggling in pairs. A bit of the front lawn came to view over the school. The BBQ pit was still smoking, fueled by two dozen neglected Bratwursts.

Off in the distance, three flaming houses lit up their neighbor-hoods with oranges and reds. Someone fired what sounded like a shotgun. Police and fire sirens wailed. Closer, little Christian rug rats ran both left and right, being chased by clowns. One bowled over the lemonade stand as a green clown dove on top of her.

"Is that part of the carnival?" Janet asked.

I shook my head, unsure what to do. It seemed a little over-whelming.

Two clowns tackled Johnny Bo's teacher. They bit her on the arm and leg then kept at it, ripping away skin with their teeth. Once well past her epidermis, they used their hands like claws and pulled on the muscles. That lifted her whole body when the mus-cles refused to give. They had to sit on her to get enough leverage to rip strings of bloody meat. One decimated a twitching arm while the other mangled a flexed leg.

The victim screamed and jacked her whole body, savagely skinning her knees and elbows in desperation to get away. It was useless; as one clown clamped his legs around her butt and upper thighs, facing her feet, he drew kicks by her free leg, but didn't seem to mind. The other clown parked himself more firmly about her neck and a shoulder, as he bent the arm out of the socket and ripped away more flesh. The clowns smacked their lips and moaned, obviously in delight.

The teacher's fingers stopped flexing, suggesting that the clown had bitten through the nerves. But the lady wouldn't die. Instead, she pleaded in every way imaginable until a rasp emerged amongst the weeping. She banged her head bloody on the playground pavement and broke fingers on her opposite hand while trying to crawl free.

All the clowns were eating people in similar fashion. Several shambled around the nine barrels that had been placed on end. Clowns ducked into the barrels and came up with little appendages between their arms and teeth, chowing down, as if they were bobbing for apples. It seemed the clowns had known enough to set the barrels upright, storing the children like pickles in barrels.

Little hands waved above the unmolested rims, reaching for someone to help them escape. At least ten adults were lying in pools of blood. Others might have fled. Every so often, an adult ran up to a barrel, tried to free a child, and got tackled for their efforts.

"Is that a Jesus play?" Johnny Bo had come up beside our frozen figures. He squinted. "I played a sheep in the Christmas play." He pointed. "This looks more like Jesus on the cross. They didn't make me do that one. It was scary."

Janet put her hand over Johnny Bo's eyes and hustled him back into the barrel. "Yes, it's a play, but we don't have a ticket. Come on, Johnny Bo, let's go for another ride through the woods."

We pushed the barrel a few feet then worked it in past an break in the bushes, hiding the whole thing.

"Now stay in there. We're doing hide and seek," Janet told him. "What are we going to do?" she asked me, the expert.

"How the hell do I know?" I felt an anxiety attack coming on. Every part of my body said, *Run!*

"We've got to save the children!" she said. Her hand clutched my arm. It trembled so much I worried she'd shake apart.

I felt powerless. I pulled her close and tried to hug away the tension. "All right, already." I took a deep breath. Thankfully, so did she. "Well, here's what I think. It looks like some kind of disease. Maybe something they all caught down at the costume store."

"Oh my God, that's right," she said into my shoulder. She pushed back a bit and looked up at my face. "Ours are homemade. So store-bought costumes make you into a zombie?"

"Yeah, something like that, or maybe a zombie bit them down at the store. Anyways, the only way to stop a zombie is to shoot it in the head or hit it with a baseball bat. I've seen about a billion movies."

"Has it come to that? I know those people. It's going to be awful, shooting one in the head. Especially since I don't have a gun."

I nodded.

She bit a lip.

As if in confirmation of the severity of the situation, several more shots rang out from the town. It remained mostly obscured by trees and walls and the water tower. A rattle of automatic gunfire added to the din of cars crashing. Closer, glass shattered, maybe a window. The lack of a Doppler shift suggested that the sirens had stopped moving.

Right about then the BBQ smoke shifted directions and plowed into my nose. My stomach said eat. Usually when I was nervous, I didn't get this hungry, but I'd been nervous since getting to my sister's place and had already missed three meals. Of course, I couldn't mention the need to eat at the moment and still have my new girlfriend.

"What do we do?" she asked.

"This is Mississippi, so where are the guns they always brag about?" I ripped off the stupid gloves on my hands. A zombie apocalypse was likely worth being able to take them off.

"The school's on cheap land, up Old Still Road. The guns are in the houses. The first one, I suppose, would be down a block and over…the Henry place on Maple Run."

"Okay, so then baseball bats?"

She yelled to Johnny Bo, "Stay in the barrel until we get back!"

I had butterflies, but took a couple of breaths.

"This way," she said, and grabbed my sleeve like it was a safety rope.

We stumbled through the trees, down the hill, somewhat toward the North end of the building. We skirted the playground mayhem and approached a half-open window, one of two dozen along the side of the school. I boosted her through, and I heard her topple into the desks and chairs. She tossed out a small chair that was almost no use, but it was just big enough to help me join her inside, though I skinned both arms in the process.

The shades were drawn. It was dark, even though it was day out, a good thing under the circumstances. We tiptoed out of the room and down the hall toward the gym. No one was in the hall, but the clutter suggested people had fled.

Just prior to the big gym entrance, we encountered the gym-office door. It was locked, so I had to elbow the window, letting a triangular piece of glass tinkle to the floor. After reaching in to unfasten the lock, we went inside. Even in the dark, I could make out the bats on the pegboard. I grabbed one—it was plastic.

"Here, try this." Janet handed me part of the leg of a badminton net's support pole. It consisted of two-inch-diameter PCV. She had the shorter piece. I put mine down because it seemed too long and light for my taste. Instead, I opted for the wooden desk. I muscled it upside down, denting the wall, and unscrewed one of its mahogany legs. It had a big screw still poking out of the fat end, but that only made it better.

We crept out the door and around the little piece of wall abutting the main double-wide entry to the gymnasium. One peek in showed it was still open to the playground via its gaping back garage door. "We need to lure them into the gym and down this dark hall, one at a time," I said.

"Good idea," she said, staring at me.

"I mean, you will have to lure them into the gym and down this dark hall."

"Why me?" she asked.

"So I can ambush them with my stick."

"Oh God, I hate that, but it makes sense." She paused a moment to grow some resolve then stoop-walked along the wall, past the trashed party decorations. I lost her behind 'pin the donkey' then caught sight as she slipped around 'dunk the clown.' The way she was doing it was taking forever.

I had time to analyze my situation. Here I was, still crushed from my last failed relationship. I didn't particularly like kids, especially if they kicked me in order to say, "Hi." She was definitely on the rebound and said she didn't want kids. Seeing through that lie had been easy by the way she'd taken care to cover Johnny Bo's eyes and jumped at the chance to save these brats.

I rolled my eyeballs. I was seriously starving now, too. If I got a headache from hunger, how would I ever manage to kill a dozen zombies? A little thing like a headache could get a person killed, what with the wincing and the not wanting to move too fast.

She crawled under the big rubber ball stand, taking her sweet-assed time. The objective was to attract them and run, not hide all the way to the huge back door. It was taking forever. I figured another three or four minutes, at least for her to make it.

The front door of the school was only down that one hall. George and the BBQ grill were ten steps past the entrance. I recalled the buns and mustard were conveniently positioned right next to the fire. I had two minutes, tops, before Janet would reach the entrance.

I decided to make efficient use of the time.

The ones on the top grill had been set aside because they were done, so I actually did a public service by taking one. I flipped the ones on the bottom, out of common courtesy. The only thing that consumed time was having to bang the mustard bottle a dozen raps to get it started. George was nowhere to be found, which figured. Not having to put up with his mouth and not garnering his help were win-lose, fifty-fifty.

I ate a third of the thing before I even got back through the front door. Halfway down the dim hallway, however, I became startled by Janet, who had spooked a zombie clown, and was now running past me, banging her pipe all over the floor and walls.

"Where the hell…?" she yelled, implying I'd not made it back, which I obviously had.

I had to toss the last bite aside. Thank God it was so dark that she likely didn't see. I concussed the first zombie clown by accident. It just kind of came out of nowhere and hit my stick. Then my eyes adjusted and five more shortened the distance between us. They weren't running, but they weren't super slow like in a Romero movie, either, so I smashed in one head and struck out after Janet.

She took a left, then another left; the school was a square after all, which wasn't good. We ended up back near the gym, having taken one too many lefts for the zombies to comprehend. Janet and I crouched beside the side door leading back onto the main floor. Likely, the half of the undead clowns who'd been eating the pesky brats were now in front eating the smoking brats, the circus-freak bastards.

I chuckled at the double play on brats.

"What could possibly be funny at a time like this?" she asked with wide eyes.

I didn't dare say what I'd been thinking, and of course I didn't mean to think that every last one of the children were brats—well, only the ones I'd met anyway—so I said, "I'm just encouraged that we led half of them off. It might be easier to free the kids, now."

She hugged my arm. Likely I'd just caused her to start ovulating.

"What's the plan?" she asked.

"Well, I think there can't be more than four or five clowns, now. We might do all right if we just charge out there and start bashing in some heads.

Her whole body jerked at the finality of that, but she stood right up before the door and put her hand on the center bar in the middle of it. One little shove and the door would open. "Okay, fine with me."

She was special. I think that was, pretty much, the moment I fell in love with her. I'd been an idiot, going for the brats like I had, instead of being diligent. I hope she never finds out.

"You've got mustard on your chin," she said.

"It's blood."

"That would be ketchup. Are you coming?"

"Well, hell, what would happen if this went on and on and became the end of the world or something? I might never get anything to eat," I said. "Then I'd pass out for lack of intake. Have you thought about what might happen if I passed out, Janet?" Then I thought better of what I'd said, so I added, "Dear. Look, I'm sorry. It was stupid. If I had to do it over again, I'd reconsider. I think all the stress got to me."

"I just asked if you were coming. Hell, the least you could have done is brought me one, too."

"Well, I was in a rush. Maybe after."

"You could have brought one for me and had yours after, don't you think?" She was stalling.

"All right, I'll go first, this time." I patted her shoulder and pushed through the door.

A clown jumped me from behind. He'd been leaning against the wall next to the door. I just barely shoved him clear before his teeth could sink into my shoulder.

I had to kick him because he came right back like he was connected to me on a spring.

Janet smacked him in the head, but the blow glanced off and her PCV rang with that aluminum-bat chink that suggested a single instead of a home run.

The clown fell, but continued to crawl after us.

We ran along the wall, toward the main gym opening we'd used last time, just hoping to get away from the one until I regained my composure from such a close call. Getting snuck up on and nearly bit had given me the willies.

"Well, well, lookie here," someone said, loud enough for me to hear. "I've been wantin' to plug my bitch's asshole brother ever since the prick drove in yesterday mornin', Rodger. Funny how things ain't social in one situuuashun, but fine in another sit…"

"Well, now's yer chance, George," Rodger chuckled.

Janet and I stumbled to a stop upon seeing the two men enter. Rodger held an over-under shotgun ready. George was pulling an ugly black Glock from his hip holster.

"Now hold your horses, George. We're not zombies." I felt the need to introduce my date. "This is Janet, by the way."

"I says you're zombies, anyways. You look like 'em," George said. "You've got blood on yer chin. Might as well plug ya' with Bessie here to make sure."

"It's mustard, you idiot. And what kind of yahoo names his Glock?" I asked.

"The Yankee's got a point, George."

"What, to hear you talk…!" George protested. "You done named your peashooter, Becky."

"Yeah, but that beaut's an Ubert 1858 Remington, George."

"Which misfires half the time. Your antique ain't half as good as this, other than the looks of it. And don't think fer a minute I ain't noticed you didn't see fit ta bring it outta your glove compartment when the need was pressin'."

Four zombie clowns jumped the idiots from behind.

This, I realized, was the favorite zombie tactic, so I spun around, and sure enough, the one that had been clubbed had gotten up and another was tagging along beside him.

Both had bright red noses and colorful wigs on their heads. I hit the tall one in the head and Janet rang the more familiar zombie with a resounding homerun that actually caved in some bone and sprinkled red rain all over our outfits.

In the meantime, both the Glock and the over-under boomed away. One bullet smacked the wall next to my head and chipped out some of the brick.

George and Rodger fell under the press of yet two more zombie clowns. Four others were on the ground, but it appeared that only one of them had taken a head shot. Clearly the fools had been doing more hunting, bar hopping and church going than watching zombie movies, as neither man had gone for a head shot.

Janet moved right up and fixed that, dispatching two undead clowns on the ground. I hit the third. By then, the colorful pair on George and Rodger were eating their jugulars.

Blood squirted as much as a couple of yards, to the pace of rapidly beating heartbeats, prompting Janet and I to back up a minute and let the poor saps squirt themselves out. We were both a mess as it is.

Then we stepped up and hit the zombies in the head. Also, we stole the dead men's guns. It all worked out pretty well in the end.

I grinned at Janet, and she smiled back and rubbed the mustard off my chin.

We turned, back to back, plugging away at the zombie clowns as they came at us from all directions. I ran out of shotgun shells after using the three shells Rodger had affixed to the stock with a shell holder, killing one zombie and nicking a few others. Janet's gun was a semi-automatic. She also seemed more practiced than me, probably because she was more of a country girl. Five clowns took the big dive before her Glock ran out.

Fortunately, that left only the two undead clowns I'd nicked. They were slow and had nasty wounds. We marched up as a team and dispatched the two stragglers with our makeshift clubs.

After scrounging through George and Rodger's pockets, we filled our guns and pockets with ammunition.

"All right, let's go save those kids." Janet faced the big, garage-type door.

The opening beckoned like a giant mouth. Janet and I stepped over the mounds of bodies, tables, chairs and wide-eyed victims, not once slipping on the blood or entrails.

Outside was more of the same. We busied ourselves shooting and bludgeoning zombies.

The last two clowns were hovering over barrels, picking out children. I shot the one in the pumpkin outfit. He'd eaten the nose and ears off a squealing boy. The last thing he did was pluck out an eyeball.

Janet finished the purple dwarf who had wrestled a head off a kindergartner. He'd pulled loose the jaw and seemed to have been going for the brain.

Then everything went quiet, except for the distant sound sirens, which had lowered in frequency, as if the patrol car batteries were dying. Somewhere across town, the reports of gunshots sounded.

Smoke lingered in thin, hazy tendrils under the slow, southern sun. One of the children moaned, then rolled over on her face and expired. Everyone else seemed dead.

Finally, a jittery weeping came to my ears and I followed the sound, coming to a barrel with a tiny child curled up in the bottom. She squeaked and hid her face in a fetal-position when my face filled the opening.

"We're never gonna get her out of there," I said.

Janet finished checking all the other barrels, ending up with an increasingly sorrowful face. "Let's roll her up the hill."

So we did. Janet helped a lot more that time. The entire time, she kept saying to the child, "We're taking you someplace safe, baby. Just be still a minute. It'll be okay."

Johnny Bo was gone. Though I was supposed to be taking care of him, to be honest, I had to force myself not to smile.

The little girl finally crawled out of the barrel. She went back in until Janet took off her clown dress, ending up in a bra and girdle. I tossed aside my wig, bloomers and dress. I turned my mom's dress inside out so I could wipe the makeup off my face. That left me in knee shorts and an *I Ate at Nancy's* t-shirt.

It was all cuddles, skin to skin, Janet and her tiny-tot toddler.

The kid wiped away her own tears, using a sleeve. She closed her eyes and puckered at me. The little angel kept it up until I leaned in so she could kiss me on the cheek.

The sweet thing had a mop of disheveled, wavy brown hair and a face full of freckles. Her mother had dressed her in a blue romper with tiny white socks and those brown Mary Janes.

Her face was full of expectation that would make a grizzly bear crawl out of hibernation.

I turned away and whispered, "Ah hell. Now I've got a sweet little crumb snatcher to feed. I'm gonna have to go down there and get us all a couple of brats."

I left the relative safety of the deep woods and stared down the hill while checking the load on my over-under. Rotten Johnny Bo was down there, kicking all the bodies, yelling for everyone to get up and pay attention to his sorry ass. I could see well into the gym from my location. The boy went in there and even jammed his own father in the nuts.

It worked. Soon, all the parents and their brood started moving. They had changed into zombies. They got up best they could, began paying attention to Johnny Bo, and then they filed into the gym.

It was the perfect diversion, because my new family was hungry. I decided to bring up the entire grill and maybe even the cooler, and God forbid I should forget the mustard.

We were hungry, and who knew how long it would take for everyone in Mississippi to turn into zombies and wander off.

We might still have to shoot some more before it was all over, and a man shouldn't have to do a thing like that on an empty stomach.

BLOOD OF A CLOWN

ANTHONY GIANGREGORIO

The evil clown let out a maniacal laugh as he slid the pliers deep into John's mouth. The tool was cold and slippery, and John could taste the metal.

The rough metal jaws of the pliers scraped against John's rear left molar, the torturer lazy, not worrying about whether or not he was pinching the tongue. The upper and lower ends of the pliers locked down on the tooth and John squeezed his eyes tight, knowing what was coming.

There was a slight pause as the maniacal clown braced himself, then there was a blinding white pain in John's head and the tooth was ripped from its mooring of twenty-five years.

Blood exploded outward from the gaping hole in his lower gum, and John let loose a blood-soaked scream that would have shattered glass, if any had been in the vicinity.

The scream was long and loud, filled with pain and suffering. In time, the screaming abated and John grew quiet once more. His lower jaw throbbed with each pulse of his heart and he felt like he was going to throw up. Bile crept to the top of his throat and he knew any second he would vomit.

His vision swam with white light as the agony that was his mouth subsided to a dull roar. When he was finally able to open his eyes, he found himself looking up at his colorful torturer.

The man was tall, well over six feet, with muscles that strained against the material of his red and yellow clown suit, which was now covered in blood splatter. John knew that it was his blood he saw.

The eyes were hidden behind dark sunglasses, which were there to protect the clown from blood spatter. The mouth was painted in red lipstick, more than an inch around the lips, the face having a base of white pancake makeup. A red ball was perched on the clown's nose and bright pink hair adorned his head. Before the torture had begun and he'd had his first glimpse of the clown, John had thought that the amalgam of color was like if a crayon box had thrown up.

The clown hadn't said a thing, only laughter escaping those painted lips and in many ways that was more chilling than if the clown had been a talker.

The clown was a true connoisseur in the art of torture, too. The instruments of bloodletting were his brushes and the human body was his canvas, and since John had found himself helpless before the clown, the silent man had done just that, each torture more creative than the last.

The clown studied the tooth in the jaws of the pliers, as small drops of blood slid from the tooth to splash onto the floor. Then, as if the tooth was nothing to focus attention on, he opened the pliers and the tooth fell to the floor. It bounced once and lay on its side, swimming in a pool of dark, congealing blood.

"Please, no more, please stop this," John whimpered, but just like before when he'd begged the torturing clown for mercy, his pleas were ignored. "Why? Why are you doing this to me?" he whispered, wanting to know the answer, but as always the dark clown who had caused him so much pain said nothing.

John looked up once more at the makeup-covered face, wishing he could at least make eye contact, but the dark glasses over the eyes hid everything, and all he could see was the hint of the orbs hiding within.

The clown picked up a four-inch long, thin stick, which reminded John of a shish-kabob skewer. Without preamble, the clown placed the skewer at the tip of John's left index finger, the pointed tip touching just under the fingernail.

As the tip touched the tender flesh under the fingernail, John yelped, knowing what was coming and ill prepared to handle it.

"Please, God, no, don't do it. For the love of all that's holy, don't do it," he begged, tears running down his blood-spattered cheeks in a steady stream.

The clown still acted like John wasn't there, as if the hand didn't belong to another human being, and with a flexing of his arm, the clown slid the skewer under the fingernail, causing John to shriek in agony. There was no way to truly describe the intense pain he felt. John thought he was going to black out, and prayed he would, but there was no mercy for him, no relief; he stayed conscious.

His entire hand and his lower arm felt like it was dipped in acid, the skewer sliding in with little difficulty, slicing through the meat of his finger. It felt like the skewer had been shoved in more than a foot, but in reality one small inch was all that had penetrated his flesh

The clown paused for a moment and went to a corner of the room, behind John. He returned a moment later with a car battery and a set of jumper cables—one end of the cables had the clamps to connect to the battery terminals, but the opposite end was missing the clamps and the exposed copper wire was plain to see.

The clown grinned malevolently and licked one of the exposed wires, then set it all down at John's feet. This was what was to come next, but for now, the clown wasn't done with the skewer, and slid it yet again under John's already inflamed fingernail.

As the white light of pain danced across his vision, John prayed for death once more.

But he knew it wouldn't come, for if his torturer wanted him dead, the sinister clown could have killed him a thousand times over already.

As John's mind swam with fog at the pain he felt, he tried once more to remember how he'd ended up in the chair of a torturer dressed as a clown.

He remembered going to the circus with a few friends to have a good time. He remembered the act where the clowns all came out, some spinning dinner plates on their hands while others pulled brightly-colored handkerchiefs from their mouths, the long streams of material seemingly endless. Alcohol had been served at the circus and John had imbibed a little too much, and when one of the clowns had tripped over his own two floppy red feet, John had catcalled and hooted in laughter, gesturing and making sure to point out to his friend and those around him what a fool the clown was.

Though he was supposed to be cheerful, the clown didn't find the humiliation funny at all, and if John had been more observant, he would have seen the anger gleaming in the eyes of the spiteful clown.

Later, when the circus had closing for the night, and John had said goodbye to his friends, he'd stumbled to into the parking lot to find his car, confident he was more than well enough to drive. He remembered reaching into his coat pocket and retrieving his keys. It was as he was about to slide the key into the door lock that he caught the hint of a colorful reflection in the side window, and then had felt hot pain in his neck, his body beginning to convulse before he passed out.

He now knew it was a taser that had been used on him.

When he'd come to, he'd found himself strapped to a wooden chair, his arms tied to each side of the arm rests, his ankles also tied to the two front legs of the chair.

It was in the same room he was in now; bleak, no windows with peeling paint, dirt on the floor, and one naked bulb hanging from the ceiling on an old extension cord. It reminded him of a small room in a warehouse, a stockroom perhaps, but each time he screamed and no one came to help him, John knew that wherever he was, no one was around to hear him beg for mercy.

He was absolutely and totally at the mercy of his captor, a man who hid his face under clown makeup.

Pulled back to a world of agony, John cried out again as the car battery sent waves of voltage into his genitals. Moving on from the skewer while John had been reminiscing, the colorfully-attired torturer had placed the exposed wires of the positive and negative ends to John's scrotum, the jagged tips biting into his flesh enough to illicit screams of agony by themselves. But then the evil clown had touched the positive clamp to the battery terminal, to let the electrical current flow to John's groin and the rest of his body, the jagged wire poking his nuts then becoming a mild nuisance in comparison.

John's body began to convulse, jerking back and forth, only the restraints on his limbs keeping him from falling out of the chair. His face turned bright red, as if he was a lobster after being been dropped into a pot of boiling water, and his eyes went as wide as diner plates, nearly popping out of his head.

His hair stood on end and the odor of cooked flesh filled the room, but John didn't notice, too caught up in a world of pain. He wet himself and was glad his pants were now lying in the corner of the room. Even as he twitched from being electrocuted, he found it ironic he would so much as give a passing thought to his pants. After all, at the moment, urine on his pants would be the least of his problems.

The clown laughed hysterically as he watched John spasming, then he removed the positive cable from the battery terminal and the current stopped.

John let his head sink onto his chest as he shook his head to clear it, saliva dripping out of the corner of his mouth to spill onto his chest. The saliva was tinted red thanks to John biting the tip of his tongue.

Electrocution was an agony there was no actual description for either. The closest thing was when a person got zapped messing with an electrical outlet but for some reason couldn't let go. If the current continued feeding into the body, as teeth chattered and limbs locked up, that was as close to a description as was possible for someone who has never actually experienced it.

The positive cable was attached again and John began to jump in the chair, his arms and legs straining at their bonds. He finally began to smell an odd odor, sweet, as if someone was cooking meat on a barbeque grill, and when he realized he was smelling himself cooking, he threw up, splashing warm vomit between his legs.

The clown jumped back so as not to have his floppy red shoes splashed with vomit, and he backhanded John with a blow that had John's teeth rattling in his mouth.

The positive cable was removed from the terminal and a heartbeat later the current ceased.

Finished with this part of the torture, the clown simply yanked at the two electrical cords that were now fused to John's scrotum thanks to the electricity that had been running through them. But the cables refused to come free, and more than a little skin went with them as they were pulled away. John yelled out once more and looked down at a pool of blood in his crotch. His balls were bleeding now and he let out long wail, as any man would do in the same circumstance.

Defiance filled him and he hissed at his torturer, spitting bloody vomit across the distance separating them from one another.

"Bastard, so help me if I get out of this fucking chair, then we'll see how tough you are!"

The clown's shoulders shook and the clown elicited a high-pitched laugh.

Having the clown laughing at him infuriated John immensely. "Don't fucking laugh at me! Why are you doing this to me! Tell me, you bastard!"

The clown didn't reply but instead walked over to a small steel table which had on its smooth surface an assortment of knifes and other implements that could be used for torturing a human being. He hovered over the scalpels, knives and needles, and John watched with wide eyes, knowing what the hand landed on would spell more suffering for him.

So when the hand landed on a simple metal spoon, such as one used with tea and biscuits on a sunny afternoon, to say John was relieved was an understatement.

"Hah, a fucking spoon? What the hell are you gonna do with that? Make me eat a bowl of soup?"

No answer was forthcoming but John still felt a surge of renewed energy. Perhaps his captor had run out of ideas and the torture was finally over.

The clown crossed the distance separating them, moving quite easily despite the red floppy shoes, and he hovered over John, gazing down on him. John could hear the air whistling in and out of the clown's nose as he breathed.

The clown reached out with his left hand and it locked onto John's forehead, pushing John's head back to the point that his neck might very well snap. John struggled to break free, but with his limbs firmly secured, he had no leverage. Desperate, he spit a glob of coagulated blood onto the clown's chest, then clacked his teeth to no avail. He still didn't know what was going to happen next, and though a silly thought, he had to admit that after everything he'd been through, to have his neck snapped now seemed very anti-climatic

He waited for what was to come next.

He didn't have to wait long.

As the clown held John's head in place, the right hand holding the spoon slowly came up and hovered in front of John's eyes. The spoon waved like a snake in a trance, moving back and forth.

Then, like a striking snake, the spoon dove downwards and the tip slid into the side of John's right eye. The metal was cold as it dug in deep, the spoon separating membranes and ganglia as it went in deep enough that the clown pulled on the handle and popped out the eye like a melon baller to a piece of cantaloupe.

On the right side of John's vision, it was like someone had flicked a light switch, the world going dark as blinding pain filled his skull. He screamed as the spoon scooped out his eye, leaving a bloody, gaping socket behind. As he screamed, the open socket touched the air and John could feel the cool air caressing the inside of the raw socket. He blinked with his remaining eye but the right side of his vision remained dark.

No sooner did he slow his screaming, the pain finally subsiding to a dull throb, then the evil clown brought back the spoon once more. The tip was now bloody, dripping with a clear fluid, and John, even in his madness, wondered where his eye had gone to. Where was it now? Had the murdering clown tossed it into the trash? Or was it in a jar with chemicals to preserve as a souvenir?

He never received an answer before the spoon was going in once more. The last image he saw was the harlequin-painted face of his captor, then the spoon went in deep and his other eye was popped out to plunge his world into darkness.

John sat in the chair, sobbing, his world nothing but darkness. He could feel the blood and ooze sliding down his cheeks from his gaping eye sockets, his eyes gone from his skull forever.

He didn't know how long he was left to wallow in misery but finally he heard footsteps and someone breathing. His head popped up and he muffled his cries, his ears now straining to pick up any telltale noise. With no sight, his nose also picked up the slack and he detected a musky smell that hadn't been there before.

It was his captor, his torturer, the demon clown, returning from whence he came; back to do more evil unto him no doubt.

"Why? Why are you doing this to me? What did I do to deserve this?" John cried out as his head fell back to his chest.

Once more there was no answer, but his head was grabbed by the hair and snapped back so his neck was exposed.

Though eyeless, he squeezed his eyelids closed, waiting for the final end, and truth be told, he now welcomed it the way a suffering cancer patient welcomed the cold embrace of death, only wanting to end the pain for good. He was in so much pain he could barely breathe and death seemed like a welcome release.

Something metallic was being picked up, he could hear the rattle on the nearby table and then he tasted metal again.

"Oh, God no, no more!" he screamed around the end of the pliers but the clown ignored his pleas and went to work once more. Like a dentist from a B horror movie, the clown was cruel beyond words. Not settling for one simple molar this time, he began tearing out tooth after tooth, John screaming as each one was ripped from his mouth in a bloody spray.

Blood and drool slid from his mouth to coat his chest in crimson and he howled in utter agony, the unbelievable pain causing him to pass out more than once.

But smelling salt aroused him each time and the torturer went right back to work. John wondered if when he passed out the clown would go grab a smoke, maybe a cup of coffee. Like a worker in an office building, he would pause and run to the smoking area, suck on a cancer stick to then run back to his cubicle and resume working again.

Time lost all meaning in his prison of darkness and agony. Days, weeks, or perhaps minutes, it all was one large entity to him now.

His captor returned when he was awake one time and the torture began anew. Even through all the pain and agony, there was the odor of the clown, a musty scent mixed with the redolence of the makeup he wore on his face.

John heard the clown pause and then the sound of a glass jar being opened. Even in his agony, John was amazed how sharp his hearing had become in such a short time. He had heard when a person lost their sight, that their other senses became stronger, more sensitive, but he'd never truly believed it until now.

There was a lull in the torture as the clown did something with the jar. John continued to move his head to the left and right, trying to pick up a telltale sound.

Then something touched his leg, something cold.

No sooner did the liquid touch him than the cold turned into searing heat that filled John from his toes to his head, as if molten lava was being dripped on him. He shrieked loudly, spitting blood and phlegm from his mouth. As he shrieked in pain, his nose detected the scent of burning meat and he quickly realized it was *his* meat he smelled.

Acid! It was acid!

Another few drops touched his other leg and he roared in agony as the acid ate into his leg, his flesh and muscle dissolving into a sticky red goo.

He kicked his legs as if he could shrug off the corrosive but it did nothing to slow the acid's descent into his limbs, and soon he couldn't even do that. The acid had eaten into his legs to the point that the nerves to control the legs had been severed.

He passed out again, but was quickly revived, and as he swooned in delirium, he heard something that had his stomach falling out from within him.

He heard his legs drop off and fall to the floor from where they had been severed from his thighs, thanks to the acid eating away at the flesh and bone.

With the wounds cauterized from the acid, he wasn't going to bleed out, and though his legs were now long gone, he swore he could still feel them.

As if it was a game, the clown picked up the legs and slapped John's face with them a few times, John feeling his own feet striking him in the cheeks to leave welts and bruises. All the while the clown laughed manically.

Just before he passed out again, he heard the sound of his legs being tossed into a corner of the room. Then he welcomed oblivion once more.

Smelling salts revived John and though technically awake, he was so out of it from the pain he could barely think straight.

Suddenly, he felt something cold slice across his left bicep and he let out a small yell. A second later, another cold slice went across his lower arm, then another and another all over his body. At first he didn't understand. Though it stung, it was certainly not as painful as the other tortures he'd received at the hands of his captor but then, as the air slowly touched the paper thin cuts, he realized what the clown had planned.

Similar to a Chinese torture, John was being cut, sliced if you will, dozens upon dozens of times. The thin cuts stung with an intensity that a simple slice from a knife could never accomplish, the razor thin slices were similar to paper cuts and each one stung a little more with each passing second until it felt like his entire body was on fire.

John didn't know how many shallow wounds he received, but he knew when the clown was finally through that John would probably go mad with the stings, as each one throbbed and pulsed with a life of its own. It was like an itch he couldn't scratch and he yelled and jumped in the chair, but he was trapped and would never get free. It's an odd feeling to know that you're completely helpless, that there's absolutely no possible chance of escape, or of help coming. That all you have to look forward to is more pain, more suffering, until the sweet release of death would be a mercy.

"Oh God, fucking kill me and get it over with, you son-of-a-bitch!" he growled, the words slurring due to him only have two of his teeth left. He did want to truly die now, of that there was no question in his mind. He was sightless, with no legs, pretty much no teeth; death would be a welcome release from the hell his life now was.

Yet, he still didn't know why any of it was happening to him. He still didn't know why the evil clown had captured him and was torturing him.

John detected the clown near him and he shifted his head, trying to hear where the man was. John quickly found out when yet another skewer was placed under the fingernail of his left thumb, the wood jammed deep, causing him to shriek loudly. Red spittle flew from his mouth and phlegm dripped from his nostrils as he cried and shook with agony.

His world was now nothing but blinding pain wrapped in a sea of darkness and he cried and screamed, switching out with each one depending on the torture.

Then, through his sobs, he heard the unmistakable sound of a blade being honed on a sharpening stone. By the breadth of the scraping blade, John knew it was long, and visions of pangas and machetes flitted through his mind.

He wondered if this was finally it. If this was the time when he would finally be released from the prison that was his mangled body. He felt something being tied around his right arm just below the elbow and a little before where his wrist was tied to the chair arm—it was rope by the feel of it. When the rope was pulled taut, he yelped but controlled his voice. He knew if he was yelling then he couldn't hear what his captor was doing to him.

No sooner did the rope grow tight then his hand began to hurt as all blood was prevented from flowing into it. The man walked away and the honing of the blade continued.

As John's hand began to throb, reminding him of how it felt when as a boy he had wrapped a rubber band around his index finger and watched the tip grow purple from lack of blood, the sharpening stopped. Then he heard footsteps and he muffled his sobs as he listened to the clown step ever closer, the red shoes slapping the cement floor with each step. Flap, flap, flap, almost comical if not for the dire circumstance John was in.

He didn't hear the blade rise into the air nor hear it fall, but he did feel it when the blade chopped off his hand at the wrist, a bolt of lightning-quick pain filling his mind, causing him to pass out as soon as it suffused his body.

When he awoke, his hand throbbed, but when he tried to move it he could feel nothing. The more he tried to wiggle the hand, the more he could feel nothing there, though the sensation of a phantom ghost limb was still prevalent.

He could hear heavy breathing near him, and just before another burst of blinding pain filled his insides like liquid fire, he realized his other arm had been wrapped in rope too, then the blade came down and the hand was lopped off to fall to the floor in a splatter of blood.

Once more he slid into unconsciousness, the overwhelming pain too much for his receptors.

John came to again, lost in a world of darkness and pain. He didn't know how long he'd been that way, but each time he passed out he hoped it would be his last, but smelling salts would always revive him.

No matter how much his captor wanted to make him suffer, there was only so long a body could survive the abuse John was receiving, and now the only defiance he had was to die, to finally spoil the fun his clown torturer was having.

But what could he do to kill himself? He was tied to a chair, no legs and no hands, sightless, what felt like a hundred stinging yet shallow wounds covering his body. Even if he lived, if right now he was saved, what kind of life would he have?

The answer was a pretty fucking terrible one.

John wracked his pain-befuddled mind to figure out some way to kill himself, but nothing came to mind.

Until one idea, though drastic as it was, finally came to him.

He didn't know if he could do it but he had no choice.

For whatever reason, the clown had left him two teeth, both at the front of his mouth. They weren't properly lined up but he shoved his tongue between them, the slippery muscle slipping out more than once.

He could hear his torturer puttering about, and he heard the sound of metal objects, that noise letting him know more pain was to follow soon. John heard a lone word uttered by the clown, the word *tongue*.

So that was next on the torture agenda. John hadn't given it much thought till then, but it appeared that the tongue had been saved for last, perhaps as the clown wanted John to be able to scream more easily so had left it in his mouth intact. But now it was time for the offending muscle to go, and no doubt it would be terribly painful.

John knew he didn't have much time if he was going to try something. He clicked his remaining teeth together, trying to catch his tongue between them, but each time the slippery muscle slid free. He could hear his captor walking toward him now, the flap, flap of the shows echoing in the room, and John let out a soft whimper as he forced his tongue between the two teeth, and with everything he had, clamped down as hard as he could

Pain flared in his head as he began to grind the two teeth together, shredding the tongue into a mangled mess. Even when the two teeth had sliced into the tongue, he opened his mouth, repositioned his tongue, then slammed the teeth together harder, as more pain filled him until he wondered if he would pass out again.

As his teeth shredded the tongue, he tasted fresh blood, a lot of it, as it began to slide down his throat. At first he tried to swallow it out of instinct, but as more and more hot blood gushed out of his mangled tongue and slid down his throat, he found he couldn't keep up.

But that was the result he wanted, after all and he finally stopped swallowing and just let it happen.

He began to drown in his own blood.

He heard the clown yell, "No!" then rush over to John and try to pry open his mouth. But with a resolve of a dead man John refused to open, though fingers probed around his lips and forced their way into his mouth.

Unable to keep his jaw shut, the fingers pried John's lips apart but the blood continued to flow, slipping out onto his chest as well as down his throat.

"No, no, you can't die, not yet! I'm not done with you!" the clown yelled in frustration.

John began to laugh as his lungs filled with blood. He was dying, and best of all, he was cheating his torturer of being the one to finally kill him. He began to cough, his breathing becoming difficult, and as the clown cut his bonds and threw him to the floor to work on him, trying to save him with CPR, John knew it was too late.

His mind was growing fuzzy and he knew this time he wouldn't awake. Despite his shredded tongue, he managed to say one last word to his captor, though he didn't expect an answer.

"Why?"

He was sliding into the dark void of death, but this time the clown replied, knowing his victim was done for.

"You laughed at me at the circus when I tripped. No one laughs at me."

"But…but you're a clown?" John managed to say, the reason for everything that had happened to him slamming into him like a ton of bricks.

In his last second on Earth, after hearing the clown's reply, John knew if he'd had just one more second, he would have laughed at the irony of it all.

That second was denied him.

CLOWN COLLEGE

MIKE CATALANO

The sun was beginning to set on the first day of the 1987 Fall semester at the Melvin White College of Clowning Arts. Having just dismissed her last class of the day, Professor Nancy Snyder closed her lesson planning book and collected a squeeze horn, squirting flower, and joy buzzer off her desk.

She placed the items in a box and carried them over to a door in the corner of the classroom with the sign *Prop Room* on it.

Nancy put the box on a shelf inside the room. Removing her wire-rimmed eyeglasses, she rubbed her eyes, then pulled out an elastic at the back of her head and let her blonde locks drape down over her shoulders.

"Gotta get used to these long hours," she yawned to herself.

At twenty-four, Nancy was the youngest professor ever to be hired at Melvin White and didn't want the rest of the staff to see her so sleepy on her first day. She ran both hands over her face and through her hair to ensure she was appropriately awake. Once satisfied, she turned toward the exit.

A clown was standing in the doorway.

"Oh God!" Nancy shrieked before composing herself. "You scared me. Do you need something from the prop room?"

The clown nodded.

"Okay, well just lock up when you're finished."

Nancy walked forward. The clown stepped out of the doorway, revealing another clown behind him.

"Oh!" Nancy hollered again. "That's not funny."

Clown #2 merely held up his palms and stepped to the side, revealing yet another clown.

"Okay, guys, cut the crap," Nancy said, beginning to get aggravated. "Class is over, so you can stop the whole act."

She marched up to the doorway but Clown #3 refused to move.

"Hey, I said enough," she said more sternly.

Clown #3 kept his gaze on her and pulled the door closed. Clown #2 stepped up beside him, creating a double blockade. Their grins were huge.

"Move out of the way," Nancy commanded. She attempted to break through them, but the clowns didn't budge, causing her to drop her eyeglasses. Nancy staggered backwards, breaking the heel on her right pump. She dropped to her knees.

"What do you want?" she asked tearfully.

Clown #1 mischievously moved his eyebrows up and down while Clown #3 began panting like a dog. Clown #2 stepped forward, crushing her glasses underneath his big, red shoe.

Nancy froze in fear. Before she could do anything, all three white-painted faces descended devilishly down on her, forcing her to the floor, their hands tearing at her clothes. Nancy tried to scream, but before she could, a colorful rag was shoved into her mouth, silencing her.

Four of Melvin White College's finest 2013 incoming freshmen sat in a circle within the prop department's classroom, rummaging through large boxes of various clown paraphernalia. The walls were decorated with smiling paper pumpkins, ghosts and witches. A couple of light blue flyers were scattered amongst the freshmen's sitting area that read, "Delta Bozo Phi's Annual Halloween Clown Jam! Be There & Be Scared! October 31st."

A pudgy, young man extracted a large party blower from a box and stood up before the others. "Check it out, guys," he said. "I can go as 'Viagra clown' tonight!" He lowered the blower to his crotch and gave the base a squeeze, causing the rolled-up tail to extend outwards.

"Really, Benny?" questioned a pale and slender girl with dark blonde hair dangling above her shoulders.

"Really, Jill?" Benny mimicked. He took a step closer to her and gave the blower another squeeze, causing it to hit her in the face.

Jill turned away in disgust.

"Benny, you know that blower's about nine inches too long," the other young man in the room commented.

"Frank, that's *not* what your mom said," Benny was quick to fire back.

The students all laughed together.

The fourth member, a girl with long brown hair, gave Benny a playful slap on the ass. "I really think you were born to be a clown," she said. "Trust me, I would know."

"Thank you, Aubrey," Benny grinned. "You really know how to make a clown smile."

"Does that mean you'll be going to the party as a happy clown tonight?" Frank asked.

"Is there really any other kind of clown?" Jill posed.

"No," Frank answered immediately, as if she was dumb for even asking. "You've got happy clown, sad clown, goofy clown…"

"Scary clown," Aubrey added.

"Scary clown?" Jill asked. "Really, Aubrey? You know I hate that stereotype."

"Stereotype or not, it's just a fact," Frank said. "Clowns can be scary. Hell, some people think that all clowns are scary. There's even a word for it. Chloro—or Clausto—something."

"Coulrophobia," Aubrey stated.

"Yeah, that's it." Frank nodded. "You're just going to have to face it, Jill, some people just really hate clowns."

"All this talk of scary clowns reminds me of that story about what happened here a long time ago, in this very room!" Benny said.

"Oh, please, Benny, must we hear about that stupid story again?" Jill rolled her eyes. "It isn't even true."

"It is so true." Benny held up a red clown nose and gave it a squeeze. "A professor got raped by ten clowns in that prop room right over there."

"Gross, stop it!" Jill covered her ears and closed her eyes. "I don't want to hear about it any more."

"It's okay, Jill," Aubrey said, putting an arm around her. "Just forget about it. Besides, Benny, it was only three clowns, not ten. Quit exaggerating."

"Whatever," Benny shrugged. "It's still a pretty fucked-up story. And try not to laugh after hearing the phrase…clown rape."

Frank covered his mouth to keep his inappropriate laughter from escaping.

Jill opened her eyes and lowered her hands. "It's not funny, it's scary. It's stories like that that make people hate what we're here to become."

"Well, that's a stereotype I aim to change!" Benny said proudly. "And it's all going to start tonight when I don my first clown costume of the year!"

"Now, I don't even think I want to go," Jill frowned.

"Don't worry, honey," Aubrey said, grabbing her box of clown gear. "The Halloween Clown Jam is an aspect of this college that's actually worth celebrating. Forget that stupid old story. Tonight's a special night for us freshman. We're unveiling our clown costumes for the rest of the school to see for the very first time. So, let's go back to the dorms and get ready."

"Oh, fine." Jill picked up her own box of gear. "This classroom's starting to give me the creeps anyway."

Aubrey gave Frank and Benny a wave. "We'll see you boys tonight," she said, escorting Jill out of the classroom.

Once the area was female free, Benny turned to Frank and asked, "You think Jill was digging my vibe?"

"Digging your vibe?" Frank smirked. "Do you mean before or after you pretended that party blower was your dick and stuck it in her face?"

"It's always the quiet, slightly insecure ones that are the biggest freaks in private."

"Just pack up your shit so we can get out of here," Frank said.

Benny began collecting his things.

"Oh and don't forget to close the door to the prop room," Frank added.

Benny trudged over to the doorway and gave the door a little kick. It swung a full ninety degrees, but it didn't close. He kicked it again, bit it still wouldn't shut.

"Fuck this," he whispered and turned away.

The two hastily exited the classroom and slammed its main door closed. The force of the impact caused the prop room door to open a little more, revealing a row of clown suits on hangers.

A pair of footsteps echoed from the hallway outside. The classroom's door was opened and the footsteps continued in. The new arrival located the ajar prop room door and rushed inside it. A pair of white-gloved hands stretched out across the hanging clown suits and yanked down a blue, one-piece with three puffy white balls down the center. In a matter of seconds, the suit was slipped on. Wearing clown makeup applied earlier, along with the suit, the identity of the new arrival was completely hidden.

"Hey, there," called a voice from the prop room's doorway.

The clown looked up to find an old maintenance man standing before a pushcart loaded with tools; he was wearing a red clown nose.

"I hope I'm not interrupting," the man continued. "I need to take a look at this door."

The clown's head slowly shook back and forth.

"Good," the man smiled, extracting a drill from his tool belt. "Don't mind me."

He turned to the door and began inspecting the hinges. The clown stepped over to a large box filled with masks. The white-gloved hands reached in and pulled out an old Michael Myers mask from the horror film *Halloween*.

"Hey, sorry to bother you again," the maintenance man said, "but could you give me a quick hand over here?"

The clown walked toward him, holding onto the Myers mask.

"I see you have your getup all set for that big clown jamboree tonight," the maintenance man said, then gestured with a screwdriver at his red nose. "This here's my little way of saluting all you clowns."

The clown halted directly in from of him and placed the mask down on the pushcart.

"Okay," the maintenance man continued, "I just want to see how the door looks when it closes. Would you just stand outside and pull it shut for me?"

The clown stepped out into the classroom and grabbed onto the door knob.

"All right, now pull it shut," the maintenance man instructed.

The clown pulled on the doorknob and the door closed all the way.

"Good!" the man called from inside the prop room. "I think we're almost done."

He opened the door and placed two fingers on the inside latch.

"Just have to see if this is going to get stuck," he said, pressing the latch.

The white gloves abruptly shoved the door closed, capturing the man's two fingers. He screamed in agony as a small drop of blood dripped from the doorknob.

The clown reopened the door just in time to see the man drop to his knees, holding his half-mangled, bleeding hand.

"Why… why?" was all he could utter.

The clown's white-gloved hand picked up a hammer from the pushcart, while the man gazed up at the blue and white costumed character, just as the hammer was swung down. The tool struck him directly on the red clown nose, the blow sending him falling instantly onto his back.

The clown took two steps closer and knelt down.

With blood gushing from his dented red nose and tears in his eyes, the man could barely see as the hammer was lifted up yet again. Bits of blood and brain matter splashed sporadically across the floor as the hammer came down repeatedly.

The clown ceased hammering once the man's eye sockets were no longer two separate holes. The white gloves, now stained a dark red, took a tool belt loaded with random sharp instruments off the pushcart and fastened it around the waist of the blue and white clown costume. The bloodied hammer was dropped into an open loop.

The clown picked up the Michael Myers mask and began yanking the auburn hair out of the top. After several cumbersome pulls, the center section of the mask's head was nearly bald. Only the hair around the outer portion remained, making it look like Larry from the Three Stooges.

The clown dipped a fingertip of a white-gloved hand into the remnants within a dust bin resting on the pushcart, then smeared a set of dark circles around the mask's eye holes.

The other gloved hand immersed itself in a dark pool of blood beside the maintenance man's crushed head. The mask's mouth region was graced by a pair of bloody fingers that smeared on a messy smile.

Once satisfied, the clown pulled on the new Michael Myers clown mask, walked out of the prop room, and closed the door.

The sun had just set behind the Delta Bozo Phi fraternity house. The structure had the look of an old-fashioned mansion with dozens of glowing jack-o-lanterns illuminating its windows. Aubrey, Benny, Jill, and Frank arrived at the base of the front porch, each dressed in their respective clown costumes.

Aubrey had on a red, ruffled skirt, white top, and a blue pig-tailed wig. Benny wore green, striped pants with a large waist that almost hid his rotund tummy, rainbow suspenders, a white tank top and red afro wig. Jill had on a pink, poofy princess dress, red and white striped tights and a flowing blonde wig. Frank wore a red and black one-piece suit and green wig with a propeller-ed beanie on top. All of their faces were covered in white makeup with random touches of red and blue.

"Well?" Benny addressed them all. "Let's go get shit-faced!"

Jill chuckled and slapped him on the butt. "Benny, what are we going to do with you?" she said and walked past him.

Benny shot an excited glance over at Frank. "See?" he softly mouthed.

Frank nodded in slightly shocked approval.

The quartet of clowns walked up the stairs of the frat house's front porch and entered the house. The inside was decorated like a psychotic big top with tented rooms, fake animals in cages with prosthetic severed body parts, and a creepy ringmaster clown with a megaphone, who walked right up to them and shouted into the megaphone, "Welcome to Clown Jam 2013! We've got thrills, cheers, and kegs of beers! Have a blast letting loose your inner clown, and don't forget to check out the Haunted Hallway up on the second floor!"

"Did you say beers, good sir?" Benny asked.

The ringmaster nodded.

"Then say no more!" Benny scooped up Jill and threw her over his shoulder. "Come on, Jill! Let's go get that beer!"

Jill screamed in delight as she was carted off down the first floor hall. The ringmaster grinned and walked off.

Frank looked over at Aubrey and said, "I guess we're on our own?"

"It definitely looks that way," she replied.

"So, what should we do now?"

"Well, that Haunted Hallway sounded pretty fun." Aubrey looked over to the center stairway leading up to the second floor. "Let's check it out."

"Very cool," Frank nodded.

The two headed upstairs.

In a small den decorated with white sheet ghosts dangling from the ceiling, the ringmaster clown poured himself a tumbler of whiskey. As he took a sip, the clown with the Michael Myers mask stepped out from behind one of the white sheets. Both white gloved hands, still stained in blood, extracted two screwdrivers—one flat head and one Phillips—from the tool belt.

The ringmaster finished his drink and turned around just as the flathead and the Phillips were both jammed into opposite sides of his neck. He dropped to his knees, his mouth hanging open, not understanding what was happening. The screwdrivers were removed, causing blood to spurt out of both puncture holes like a lawn sprinkler. The ringmaster's eyes rolled upwards as he flopped over onto the floor.

In the back area party room of the house's first floor, Benny and Jill were immersed within a carnival of alcoholic anarchy. There were clowns doing keg stands, clowns playing beer pong, and clowns taking shots. A small room in the far left corner housed a bar complete with a barkeep clown, who would ring a bell when someone's drink order was ready.

Benny held up a red plastic cup of beer towards Jill and said, "Okay, on your mark, get set, go!"

The two started chugging their beers at an incredible rate. Benny took a fleeting glance at Jill to see that she was actually keeping up with him. He tilted his head back a bit more, causing his beer to go down the wrong pipe. Jill's white makeup covered forehead was hit with a wet spray of beer as Benny coughed and dropped his cup.

"Aw, Benny!" she exclaimed, wiping off her face.

"I'm… sorry!" Benny exhaled between coughs. "I think I just shot beer out of my nose."

Jill covered her eyes and started cracking up. Benny breathed a sigh of relief.

"I think if you're ever hired for a fraternity party, you should do that in your act," she smiled.

"Nice idea!" Benny grinned. "Maybe we could be a double act. I didn't know you could chug like that."

"There's plenty of things you don't know about me. So why don't you go get me another drink while I go clean this beer off me?"

"You got it!" Benny rushed off to the keg while Jill walked out of the back room and into the hallway that led to the front, where the bathroom was located. Before entering, she caught sight of the ringmaster clown being dragged towards the front door by the Myers clown. With a laugh, she shook her head and went into the bathroom.

Outside of the frat house, a new group of clowns walked onto the front porch, but before they could knock, the front door opened and the Myers clown came forth, hauling the bloody ringmaster. The group of clowns burst into a fit of Halloween-spirited laughter and walked into the house.

The Myers clown propped the ringmaster up on a beach chair on the side of the porch, like a scary decoration, then reentered the house, kicking the front door closed on the way in.

Meanwhile, up on the second floor, Frank emerged from a very dark hallway near the end of the Haunted Hallway tour. A row of black lights on the ceiling caused his white face to glow eerily.

"Aubrey?" he called out. "Are you there?"

An answer wasn't returned from the darkness.

"Hey, Aubrey!" Frank yelled.

"I'm here!" a voice called back and moments later, Aubrey came out into the black light. "It was so dark in there," she said. "We got separated."

"I know," Frank replied. "I was only worried for a second."

"Aw, did the Haunted Hallway scare you?"

"Oh, yeah, it was terribly scary," Frank joked.

"I'm surprised there aren't any scary clowns up here," Aubrey laughed.

"Aubrey, we're all dressed as clowns," Frank stated. "I doubt any of us are scared of them."

"Good point. I guess I was remembering that 'some people just really hate clowns' speech you gave this afternoon."

"Sorry if that got under your skin; then Benny started telling that stupid story about the professor."

"Oh, it isn't a story," Aubrey assured him. "I know that really happened and I'm not scared of it."

"You're one brave clown," Frank smiled.

Back downstairs in the party room, Benny and Jill were about to complete their third chugging contest.

Jill finished first and pounded her red cup down on the table. "Done!" she shouted.

Benny swallowed his last gulp and lowered his cup and head in shame.

"You're amazing," he marveled. "A beautiful princess clown, who can drink like a pro."

Jill threw down her cup and grabbed Benny's face. Clearly feeling the buzz of the chugging contest, she planted a kiss square on his lips. Benny's eyes went wide in shock, but eventually closed in acceptance. The two pulled away simultaneously and stared at each other in silence.

"Okay," Benny nodded with enthusiasm. He scooped Jill up once again and darted towards the nearest door, then flung it open to reveal a descending staircase. "Looks like it's the basement for us." He began going down.

His motions were observed from afar by the Myers clown, who was standing quietly in a corner of the room.

Once Benny had disappeared down the stairs, the eyes behind the dark circles of the white mask gravitated toward the room with the bar in it. The Myers clown began walking in that direction.

None of the partygoers gave a second look at yet another clown amongst them.

Once the Myers clown exited the party room, Frank walked in without Aubrey. He noticed a vacant beer pong table and began setting it up with some plastic cups.

Downstairs in the basement, Benny dropped Jill down on a random couch and got on top of her. He leaned in close to kiss her.

"I'm not sure we should be doing this," Jill whispered.

"Oh, I think we should," Benny replied. "I'm going to be very gentle."

"But what if somebody comes down here?"

Benny looked around the empty basement. "I don't think anyone's coming down here," he said. "There isn't any beer down here."

Jill laughed. Taking her merriment as a green light, Benny kissed her with a touch of passion.

She started to grab the back of his head, but abruptly pulled away. "I don't think I can do this," she said, tightly closing her eyes.

Benny lowered his head.

"I know I'm not the thinnest of guys, but…" He sighed, thinking she was referring to his weight.

"Oh, no, no." Jill shook her head. "That's not what I mean. It's just that… I… I have my period."

Benny's mouth hung open for a moment.

"Yeah, that's probably why I was acting so bitchy earlier today," Jill confessed.

Back upstairs in the room with the bar, the barkeep clown was wiping down the beer-soaked countertop when he felt something graze his ankle. He looked down to see the Myers clown sprawled out on the floor and aiming a nail gun upwards.

Suddenly, the barkeep's head shot backwards as a piercing nail struck him right between the eyes. He dropped to the floor so fast that no one noticed, the sound of the nail gun lost in the noise of the party.

Moments later, the bar's bell rang out through the party room. The majority of the partygoers filed into the room as chants of "Shots! Shots!" began filling the air.

They were met at the counter by the Myers clown, holding a large tray of shot glasses filled with a light green liquid.

The tray was set down and the partygoers made certain not a single glass was left behind.

The Myers clown pushed a half empty box of drain cleaner into an opened cupboard and casually walked out from behind the bar.

Down in the basement, Benny was seated upright next to Jill. "Did I come on a little strong?" he asked. "Sorry 'bout that, if I did."

"No, it's fine," Jill replied. "I shouldn't have let it go as far as it did."

"Well, we don't have to go that far. I mean, I don't always go all the way on the first date. What do you think I am, some kind of slut?"

Jill let out a hearty chuckle.

Benny stood up. "Just wait here a sec," he said. "I've gotta use the bathroom, but I'll be right back. Then we can try and get back to business."

"All right," Jill nodded.

He walked off, past the stairway and entered a small bathroom located on the other end of the basement. He flipped on the light and extracted a wallet from his green-striped pants. Reaching inside the billfold, he pulled out a condom wrapper.

"Period or not, I'm going in," he grinned quietly and tore open the wrapper.

As Benny was about to apply the prophylactic, there was a soft knock on the door. Startled, he dropped the rubber to the floor. "Hey, I'm almost finished, Jill," he called out.

There was a second, slightly louder knock.

"Really?" Benny grinned. "Okay. Knock twice if you want to come in here and do it."

The door received two knocks.

Benny excitedly scooped up his condom and opened the door, only to have a handsaw immediately slash through his stomach. Benny didn't scream, his mouth locked closed, as he looked up at the Myers clown staring silently at him.

He then glanced down at the blood gushing out of his waist, not understanding what was happening.

In a fit of pained confusion, Benny trudged forward. The Myers clown stepped out of the way, allowing him to move awkwardly back towards the other side of the basement.

"Is that you, Benny?" Jill called out from the couch. "I thought I heard a noise before."

Benny was unable to reply, but continued plodding toward her.

"Benny?" she called again. "Are you there?"

Benny finally rounded the stairway and came into view. Jill gasped at her first sight of the blood on his stomach that had now dripped down and was seeping through the crotch area of his green-striped pants.

"What the hell, Benny?" she exclaimed. "Are you making fun of me for having my period?!"

He said nothing, but kept walking closer.

"You're making fun of me for having my fucking period!" Jill went on. "I can't believe you!"

She jumped off the couch and marched at him. He opened his mouth to plead for her assistance but nothing came out, so he reached out his hand for help. Jill ignored the gesture and shoved him aside. He tumbled to the floor hard, still bleeding profusely.

"Asshole!" she yelled and headed for the stairs.

She was halfway up the steps when a sharp, searing pain burst through her right foot. Jill screamed and look down to find a bloody nail sticking up out of her foot. She tried lifting her heel, but couldn't remove it from the step.

"What the fuck?" she cried, as tears formed in her eyes from the pain.

She placed her left foot on the next step in order to get some leverage, and a nail was promptly shot through that foot too. Jill howled in pain and lost her balance.

She began falling backwards, but her crucified feet still wouldn't budge. The force of her descent caused both ankles to snap. The back of her head cracked on the edge of a step and her blonde wig fell off.

In an aching daze, Jill gazed up as the upside down visage of the Myers clown came into view. The bloody white-gloved hands grabbed her wig, slammed it back onto her head, then sent two nails shooting down into her eyes.

Jill's body bucked once as the nails penetrated her brain, then she went still.

Back upstairs, Frank waited patiently in the empty party room beside the now fully-setup beer pong table.

Aubrey entered the room from the front hallway.

"There you are," Frank said.

"Yeah, sorry I took so long," Aubrey replied. "Just girl issues, ya know? Jill and I are so close, we're both actually on the same cycle."

"Whoa!" Frank held up his hands. "Too much info! You can take as long as you want! I put together some beer pong action. Why don't we play and forget you ever mentioned what you just said."

"Okay," Aubrey laughed and walked to one end of the beer pong table. "Boy, this party sure seems to have died down."

"Yeah, they all went into the bar for some shots. I didn't bother because I knew we were about to beer pong it."

"So, are you telling me you're expecting to lose?" Aubrey smirked. "You know, the loser is the one who drinks the most."

"Well, maybe I was just planning on being nice and letting you stay in the game?"

"I guess we'll see. Rack 'em up."

Aubrey grabbed three ping pong balls and began juggling them.

"If I complete one behind the back pass, I go first," she said, concentrating on the small white orbs. "Deal?"

"Okay," Frank nodded. "Deal."

Aubrey smiled and began tossing the balls higher. Upon reaching her desired juggling height, she flung her arm behind her back and flipped a ball up and over her shoulder. With a little squat, she caught the ball in her other hand and completed one final juggling round.

"Holy shit!" Frank marveled. "How did you do that?"

"Balance, coordination," she said, catching all three balls in her hands. "Or the fact that I truly was born to be a clown."

"You definitely do have the skills. Now, let's see how you apply them to beer pong."

Aubrey let her first ping pong ball fly and sunk it in one of the plastic cups before Frank. He quickly guzzled down the beer and watched as her next shot also splashed down for a score. He then went on to sink his first two shots, thus keeping the score tied and the beer flowing.

The match went by rather fast with both Aubrey and Frank displaying highly accurate shooting abilities. Before long, they were both down to just one cup each.

"Okay, girlie, the pressure's on," Frank said. "Sink or swim. Or sink or drown, whatever."

Aubrey burst out laughing. Clearly, the quick consumption of alcohol was having an effect on them.

"You know, Frankie, I wasn't expecting you to be this good," Aubrey chuckled.

"I'd like to see you try and juggle those balls now," he grinned.

"Oh, I bet I could still do it. It doesn't matter how much beer I've had." She casually lined up her final shot. "Clowning for me is innate."

"Innate?"

"Yeah, you know, like I was born with it." Her eyes oddly began to well up with tears.

"Hey, Aubrey, I'm sorry if I said something wrong," he said, sobering up a bit.

"No, it wasn't you," she said. "It was never you. It's always been me."

"I don't understand."

Tears tolled down her cheeks. "That professor we were talking about today," she continued. "The one who was attacked… the one who was raped."

"Yeah, but why would you bring that up?"

Aubrey lowered her head and wiped her eyes. "It really did happen. Three clowns raped my mother and made… me." She let out a strange, unwilling laugh. "Pretty funny, huh?"

"Whoa, hold on," Frank said. "Why are you messing with me? Did Benny put you up to this?"

"No, I wish," she sniffed. "I thought embracing my skills instead of trying to shun them would help me and my mother, sort of, overcome the past."

"So the reason you're such a good clown is because you're the daughter of three clown maniacs?" Frank huffed. "Stop messing with me. I don't like it."

Aubrey looked at him straight away, unable to contain her tearful sobbing.

"Holy shit," he whispered. "I…I need a drink."

He rushed off while Aubrey attempted to compose herself.

Frank took one step inside the bar room and at once halted in his tracks.

His limbs froze and his eyes bugged out wide. The floor was covered in motionless clowns with blood foaming from their mouths.

"What the…" he stuttered. "What the fuck's going on?" He instantly whipped out a cell phone from a hidden pocket in his costume and dialed 9-1-1. His body was shaking. "Hello," he said into the receiver. "Please, come right away to the Delta Bozo Phi house. People are… dead. I…"

A hand tapped him on the shoulder. Frank dropped the cell phone and spun around to find Aubrey there.

Confusion emanated from her moist eyes. "Frank, I… what's happening?"

Something within her stare didn't sit well with him. "You, Aubrey?" he said. "Why would… is this some sort of sick vengeance for you? For your mother?"

"Frank, please," she said, "I don't want you to…"

"Stay away from me!" he shouted and took a step back.

"Frank, just wait a second."

"Stay away!" He took another step back and tripped over one of the poisoned clowns on the floor, landing on his back amidst a pile of brightly-colored bodies.

One of the prone clowns suddenly turned and looked directly at him. Frank yelled in shock as the Myers clown sat up and jammed the pointed tip of a cordless power drill into his forehead.

Before Frank could do or say anything, the bloody white-gloved hand squeezed the trigger and sent the drill spinning. Bits of blood and flesh sputtered across Frank's face as the drill bit was shoved all the way down.

His legs kicked about briefly before succumbing to his brain's punctured transmitters.

The Myers clown stood up, leaving the drill stuck in Frank's head, then turned to face Aubrey. She had her hands covering her mouth and couldn't move. The Myers clown extracted a small wood saw from the tool belt and began walking toward her.

"The police will be here any minute," she warned.

The Myers clown continued getting closer.

"Get out of here right now!" Aubrey shouted, still unable to move.

The Myers clown grabbed her wrist just as red lights began flashing through the fraternity house's windows. Aubrey gasped as the wood saw swung down and sliced her forearm, leaving a shallow wound behind; blood seeped from it and dripped to the floor

"Go!" she screamed. "The police are here! There's a back door in the other room. Just leave!"

The Myers clown stared directly into her eyes. Aubrey watched as the red lights bounced off the pale white mask.

The wood saw was abruptly returned to the tool belt. The clown rushed into the party room and exited through the back door.

Holding her dripping forearm, Aubrey pressed her back against the bar room's wall and slid to the floor. A fresh set of tears rolled down her face.

Roughly a half hour later, the Delta Bozo Phi house was swarming with police, paramedics, and coroners.

Aubrey was seated on a small couch in the party room. Her eyes were focused on the floor as a paramedic finished dressing the cut on her forearm.

"Okay, you're all set," the paramedic said and stood up. "I'm so sorry you had to go through this."

"Some people just really hate clowns," Aubrey murmured, still looking down.

The paramedic walked away and was replaced by a police officer, who pulled up a chair before Aubrey.

"Hello, miss, my name's Detective Williams," he said. "Is there anything I can get you? Water? Coffee?"

Aubrey shook her head.

"We need to contact your parents," the detective continued.

"It's just my mom," Aubrey answered. "But she's not home."

"Okay, do you know where she is?" He took out a notepad and pen. "She must be worried sick about you."

DEAD IN THE BED

DANIEL LOUBIER & BRIAN J. ORLOWSKI

Bethany Travers was excited.

Driving home from school towards a much needed four-day weekend, she sang along with the *10,000 Maniacs'* song, *Because the*

Night, as it blared over the Honda's radio. She'd just endured the tumult of midyear exams, and after two weeks of cramming, the upcoming mental break promised a respite that at one time seemed more like a mirage—a hazy-looking oasis that stood between college and home. The mirage, however, was now a reality, and she looked forward to forgetting her studies and spending time with friends who'd gone away to other schools.

Only two years removed from high school, Bethany greatly valued the time spent with old friends. She enjoyed college plenty and had made many good, new friends, but they weren't the ones she'd grown up with. They weren't the ones who knew her inside and out, who could predict what she was going to do or say next. In a way, her old friends were like family and her new friends were…friends.

A tiny light flickered just past her elbow as she sped along Interstate 91. She glanced down into the small tray below the radio. Her cell phone was on silent mode; the only indication of an incoming call was the fully-lit LED screen.

Dummy, she thought. *Why didn't I turn the ringer on? Good thing I saw it light up.*

She picked up the phone. The name Charlotte showed on the screen. She pressed 'send' and held the phone to her ear.

"Charlie!" she yelled. "What's up, you dirty whore?"

"Who are you calling a whore, you filthy slut?"

Charlotte and Bethany laughed at each other for several seconds before Charlotte spoke again. "Where you at? Are you close?"

"Yeah," Bethany said. "I'm just passing…" she paused to look at the oncoming exit sign. "Exit sixteen. I should be home in like twenty minutes."

"Sweet."

"Where are you?"

"I'm with Emma and Crystal," Charlotte said. "We're at For-ever 21 trying on some costumes."

"Ha-ha!"

When the two were freshmen in high school, Bethany and Charlotte felt 'older' whenever they shopped at the trendy retailer. They felt as if wearing the clothes made them look more like high school seniors. When they eventually *became* seniors, the novelty wore off and Charlotte took to referring to the store's overly-flashy and figure-hugging apparel as 'costumes' rather than traditional wear. On one hand, it made Charlotte seem hypocritical, but on the other, Bethany loved how her best friend never took life too seriously.

Suddenly, the car jumped in the middle of the lane; the front wheel had struck a pothole, jarring the phone from Bethany's hand.

"Shit!" she yelled.

"Bethany!" Charlotte called out. Bethany could hear her friend scream into the phone as she leaned forward and reached blindly for the floor beneath the steering wheel.

"Bethany!"

"One second!" Bethany called out. Her fingers rolled over the floor mat, eventually gliding over the device. She plucked at it with her finger and thumb, then brought it to her ear.

"Hey!" she said, sounding out of breath.

"What the f…"

"Sorry," she cut off her friend. "I just slammed a pothole or something. My phone slipped out of my hand."

"Ah," Charlotte said, her voice now less distressed. "Gotta love those Massachusetts' highways in the winter."

"Ha, yeah…something like that."

"Well anyway, bitch, you gonna call me when you get in?"

Bethany smiled. "Yeah, I'll give you guys a call when…"

The car jumped again. This time, there was no pothole. The tire blew open and pieces of rubber exploded past the passenger window. The car immediately began pulling to the right and Bethany fought to correct the vehicle. She could simultaneously hear the metal rim grinding against the asphalt, and Charlotte again yelling on her end of the phone.

"Hey! What the hell! What happened now? Are you okay?"

Bethany wasn't able to answer as she wrestled the Honda. She gripped the steering wheel and leaned to her left as the car stubbornly careened off to the right, but eventually, the damage to the tire proved too much. The bald rim caught the rumble strip, disorienting the car even more. The harsh vibration caused the steering wheel to spin in Bethany's hands, turning on its own until the car swerved sideways.

That's when the car took flight.

The combination of the wintry road and the blown tire caused the Civic to flip on its right side. It then rolled onto its hood, over to the driver's side, and then back on its wheels. It rolled several more times, out of the lane and off the highway, into a large windbreak of trees, where the car finally rested on its side.

B ethany woke up in a strange, darkened room. Her head was foggy and she felt exhausted, as if she'd been asleep for a day but still needed to sleep for two more. A constant *beep, beep, beep* to her left eventually grabbed her attention.

She tried turning her head, but stopped when excruciating pain forced her to remain still. She clenched her fists and gritted her teeth against the pain. She breathed deeply, tried to turn her head again, slowly this time.

She kept turning until she began to cross the pain threshold. Her eyes found the heart monitor and she realized where she was.

I'm in a hospital.

She looked down at her bed and tried to shift her legs under the sheets. Another lightning bolt shot through her—this time in her right leg—and she groaned. Something was definitely wrong. She was injured, and by the looks of things, considerably so.

Although the room was dimly lit, Bethany was able to see it was quite vast. She could also see other beds with patients in them.

I must be in some kind of intensive care, she thought. A form slumped over in a chair next to her bed. She recognized her mother and tried to speak to her, but her voice was muted. *What the hell!*

A disturbance from across the room caught her by surprise. There was nobody walking around, at least no one she could see. She tried searching out the source of the noise as best she could. A small figure walked through the middle of the ICU. The figure was male and the size of child and yet, his hair was curly and thick around the sides but bald on the top. He wore a strange outfit, too: puffy shirt—it was too dark to determine color—big suspenders, big, billowy 'balloon' pants; and large, round-footed shoes.

Bethany tracked the small figure as he flitted from patient to patient, like a bee moving flower to flower, seemingly searching or examining each unconscious body. She tried to speak again, to get the person's attention, but her words only came out in cracked whispers. The little person continued walking along until finally stopping at the foot of a patient's bed.

Bethany watched with curiosity as the person moved closer to the unconscious patient. The figure was so short that its head barely reached the mattress.

Can't be a doctor, Bethany thought. *Maybe a relative?*

While Bethany tried to figure out the nature of the little person's presence, the small figure did something Bethany never expected. It jumped up onto the bed and straddled the sleeping patient.

What the...

An overhead light cast enough of a glow that Bethany could now see the figure more clearly. The face was white, as if painted, and the half-balding hair was even more wild-looking in the relatively superior light. The figure's shirt was multi-colored and Bethany also noticed that the shoes were bright red. The final detail that caught Bethany completely off guard was the round red nose.

What? A clown?

The clown turned his head in Bethany's direction. She inhaled sharply, startled by the clown's sudden awareness that she was watching him. She couldn't see the eyes from this distance, but a nasty, evil grin curled up the sides of his face. So filthy was his stare that Bethany began to feel sick. The clown then brought a small, white-gloved hand to his throat. In his tiny fingers, he wielded a scalpel.

Bethany narrowed her eyebrows, confused, as the clown then pantomimed a slicing motion from ear to ear.

Bethany's eyes went wide. *Oh my God!*

The clown then turned back to the patient under his small frame, raised the scalpel over his head, and brought the blade down into the person's chest. He pulled out the blade and buried it in the patient again and again.

Bethany stared in silent shock as blood sprayed up from the patient's torso. She again tried to force her voice to her lips but to no avail. The wet, crunchy sound of the scalpel entering the patient's flesh, though at a distance, was nauseating. Bethany tried to move her hands, her arms, anything that might wake her sleeping mother, but the sedative her doctors had given Bethany rendered her limbs useless.

She looked around and tried to find…something. A small square device lay on the bed by her hand—a red, circular button. Bethany was able to lift her hand and rest it on the red button. To her dismay, she didn't hear any alarm; no buzzers or ringers off in the distance to indicate her message was being received by any staff. When she looked back to the clown, she watched him continue his bloody massacre. He cackled maniacally, his face split into a malevolent grin.

She raised her hand again and pressed the nurses' call button over and over.

"Okay, I'm coming," a voice called.

Someone was coming!

Oh, thank God! Bethany saw her mother shift in the chair; she was waking up.

"I hear you," the voice said again. A woman with brown hair and an honest face appeared at the end of Bethany's bed. She smiled. "Well, hello," the woman said softly, assumingly so as not to wake the other patients. "Good to see you awake."

Bethany didn't have time to return the polite gesture. She motioned over to where the clown had been murdering the other patient, only he was gone. The clown had disappeared!

The body was still there, though. Blood oozed from numerous wounds as loose bits of flesh fell to the floor.

"Oh no!" the woman cried. She ran to the bleeding patient.

Bethany's mother, now awake, turned to see what had happened. She brought a hand to her mouth as her eyes met the bloody carnage across the room. "Oh my God!"

"I need some help in here!" the woman called out. "Get me a code cart! We have a Code Blue!"

Light flooded the entire room and more people wearing hospital scrubs ran past Bethany and her mother. Bethany slammed her hands against the mattress, desperate to get someone's attention. She again tried to say something. This time, she was able to force out a loud whisper: "He killed 'em! He killed 'em!"

Bethany's mother turned around at the sound of her daughter's strained voice.

"Bethany! What is it?" Her mother immediately began to look her over. "Are you hurt? Where is it? Where does it hurt?"

Bethany strained and continued to shout in whispers until the engine in her throat finally started to turn over. "Someone killed that person! He stabbed them!"

Bethany's mother shook her head. "Someone stabbed that person? Who? Where is he?"

More hospital staff ran past, but another nurse stopped when she saw Bethany was awake. She saw the terror in both Bethany and her mother's eyes and ran around the bed to pull the privacy curtain.

"I'm so sorry you had to see that. Let me get this for you," the nurse said quickly.

"No!" Bethany shouted, her voice even stronger now. "Someone killed that person!"

"Who?" her mother asked.

"Who was it?" the nurse asked.

"It was a small person! He was dressed like a clown! I watched him stab that person!"

Bethany's mother, and the nurse, stood in silence. They both eyed Bethany cautiously.

Then, her mother's face broke from concern and into pity. "Oh, baby…"

"Mom, I saw him! He was a little clown, and he stabbed that person!"

"Okay," the brown-haired nurse said. "I need you to try to calm down. It's dark in here and I'm sure your mind is just playing tricks on you."

"No!" Bethany shouted. "I saw a little man dressed as a clown. He walked by my bed and went and killed that person!"

The nurse's concern seemed to grow congruent with Bethany's agitation. "All right." The nurse turned to Bethany's mother and very evenly said, "Try and keep her calm. I'll come right back with a sedative." She looked out into the maelstrom of nurses and doctors rushing around the ICU, and picking her moment, dove into the melee.

Bethany tried to watch around the curtain as the staff cleaned up the incident. They covered the body with a blanket and wheeled it off. Janitorial people came in and started cleaning the floor. The nurse suddenly returned with a syringe and inserted the sedative into Bethany's IV bag. Bethany looked over at her mother, and at the overwhelming sadness and fear that twisted her mother's face.

"Mom…" Bethany mustered. "It really was…"

The sedative started to kick in and Bethany felt her mother's concerned hand take hers just as the veil of sleep covered her and gently closed her eyes.

"Hallucinations? How?"

"Any injury to that part of the brain could cause someone to believe they're seeing something that's really not there."

Bethany woke up again. This time the room was much brighter. Her mother stood at the end of her bed, opposite a man wearing a white lab coat—a doctor.

"Mom," Bethany said with great effort.

Her mother turned. "I'm here, baby. I'm here." She hurried to Bethany's side and took her hand. She squeezed it hard and said again, "I'm here."

"Mom, what happened?" she asked as the doctor walked around the other side of the bed.

"You were in a car accident, Bethany," her mother said.

Confused, Bethany said, "No…I know that. What happened to the little clown?"

Her mother opened her mouth to speak but she stopped. Her eyes pleaded with the doctor for assistance.

"Hi, Bethany," the doctor said in a soft tone. "I'm Dr. Raimi. I performed your surgery last night. You weren't awake when we received you in the E.R. Your injuries were pretty significant and we had to rush you into surgery. You suffered multiple fractures in your right leg, along with some ligament damage. We were able to repair quite a bit, but we're going to need you to stay here so we can monitor you, and ultimately, perform a second surgery, which will hopefully be the final one. I'm confident you'll be walking again very soon. However, your mother and I were discussing a CT scan of your head."

He held up a small tablet computer showing multiple versions of what looked like the same overhead black-and-white X-ray image of—Bethany assumed—her head and brain. He pointed to a dark, oval-shaped orb inside the brain.

"This is the temporal lobe," he began. "It appears this part of your brain was injured during the accident. Swelling or trauma to that part of the brain has been known to cause any number of issues. Manifestation from such an occurrence can alter personality and affect behavior, impair long-term memory, cause disorders of visual perception, and disturbances of auditory sensation and perception—basically issues of the mental or cognitive sort."

Bethany was stunned. They thought she was making it all up, that a bump on her head was responsible for the mass hysteria that occurred in the hospital the previous night. It was absurd.

"You're telling me I didn't see any of that? You're saying this ICU was not in a panic last night?"

"Oh, there was definitely some chaos here," Dr. Raimi said. "Just not the kind you're thinking."

Bethany scoffed. "So the patient in that bed over there…" She motioned with her hand. "Was *not* stabbed and bleeding last night?"

Dr. Raimi softened his tone even more. "That patient had severe lacerations across her torso. Her stitches tore and she bled out. She must have moved in her sleep, unfortunately."

Bethany shuddered as a visceral image entered her mind.

"Her wounds were too serious to overcome," he continued. "Her closures didn't hold and she bled out last night. I'm very sorry you had to see that."

Bethany was quiet. All at once she was trying to process Dr. Raimi's explanation and think of a rebuttal.

Each time she thought she'd found a flaw in his account, she recognized how very possible—and likely—it was. The doctor's explanation made perfect sense. But the clown seemed so *real*. Bethany swore she felt its presence, its existence.

She wanted to believe that what she heard and what she saw were completely genuine. She simply didn't want to accept what the doctor had told her was true.

"Well how long will this last?" Bethany's mother asked.

"For now, we don't know, unfortunately. But we'll continue to monitor her scans and do some further testing tomorrow, as well as allow her enough time to recover from the first leg surgery before we go in for the second one." Dr. Raimi turned to Bethany and rested a hand on her forearm. "For now, you should try to rest. Last night was certainly traumatic enough for you without having to witness the death of a patient. For that, again, I am sorry."

A fog rolled over her eyes and Bethany could only nod weakly as the doctor walked away. She *had* seen a small figure stabbing that patient last night. Hadn't she?

Maybe what the doctor had told her was true; maybe it was all a symptom of her head injury, but Bethany couldn't simply dismiss the clown as a trick of her mind.

She looked up at her mother who remained by her bed, seeing the worry on her mother's face.

"Mom?"

Bethany's mother flinched, caught mid-thought, and met her daughter's eyes.

"Am I going crazy?"

"My baby…" Her mother reached her arms around Bethany's shoulders and leaned in to her. "It'll be all right." Then, after a few seconds' pause, she said, "It's nothing permanent."

Bethany's heart deflated.

"So you believe the doctor? That it's all in my head?"

"Shhh, now. Don't let it worry you." The weakness in her mother's voice did nothing to soothe Bethany's anxiety. "You just get some rest now." Her mother reached for the remote control on the bed sheet. "Want to watch something? I'm not even sure what's on TV this time of day. I'm never…"

"No, thanks," Bethany said. She looked away from her mother and rested her head on the pillow. "I just want to lay down for a while."

"Oh…okay." Her mother awkwardly looked for a place to put down the remote, ultimately settling on the same spot on the bed. "I'll leave the remote here. I'm going to go get some tea. Would you like something?"

"No, thanks."

Her mother hesitated for a moment, but left without another word. Bethany stared at the light-blue curtain that separated her bed from the patient next to her. Her mind continued to race, and she focused on the din of the ICU: machines beeping and pumping, IV poles wheeling about, patients coughing and moaning, and doctors, nurses, and visitors constantly moving around the unit.

The noise all slowly melded together as Bethany's focus waned.

She had nearly dozed off when she saw the terrible eyes and nasty grin of the little clown staring into her face.

When she opened her eyes, she was still in the ICU. It was still the same day and her mother had left only minutes ago.

Bethany felt rested.

She'd slept much of the day, having woken up only to eat a flavorless dinner provided by the hospital, and to look at images of her wrecked car. Her mother had taken pictures to show the insurance company.

"They're trying to say you lost control," her mother said. "That it's your fault." Then she'd shown Bethany a picture of a gaping hole in the road. "Here's a pothole about fifty yards from where your car stopped." She showed Bethany a close-up of each of the Honda's four tires. Three of the tires were clearly in much better condition than the fourth. The fourth tire was shredded down to the rim. "This," her mother continued, "is the front passenger-side tire. It's obvious the tire was destroyed, which is what caused the accident."

Her mother continued on and on about Bethany's case against the insurance company. She even stopped several passersby—

hospital workers—to ask their opinion of the photographs and whether they thought Bethany had a solid case.

Most politely declined, claiming not to have any good legal advice. At Bethany's insistence, her mother finally put away the pictures and let the issue rest.

Now it was the middle of the night. Bethany felt revived and far more awake than she had when she woke up the previous night.

Her leg ached and she wondered if her pain medication had begun to wear off. She thought about pressing the nurses' call button to have someone come check on her meds, but decided against it.

I can push through this pain, she thought. *This is nothing.*

The chair by her bed was empty. Her mother had gone home to walk their two golden retrievers hours ago.

They'd been cooped up by themselves at home all day, and while both dogs had long ago been housebroken, Bethany was quite certain their bladders were likely to give way soon, if they hadn't already.

Her mother wanted to call a neighbor so she could stay at the hospital, but Bethany insisted she was fine. She even suggested her mother sleep at home tonight.

"You look like crap, Mom."

"Look who's talking."

Bethany laughed. "Nice. But seriously, you should go home. You need some real rest. I'll be fine."

Her mother regarded her curiously. "Well, that's the first time I've heard you laugh so...I guess." She waved a stern finger at Bethany. "But if *anything* happens, I want someone to call me."

"I promise; you'll be the first number they dial."

"Okay." Her mother reached in for a hug, then backed off quickly. "Are you sure? I can call George, he knows where the hide-a-key is, he can let…"

"Go, Mom! I'll be fine. I swear."

"Okay. I'll go. I'll give your dad a call, too. I'm sure he's waiting for an update."

"Where is he?"

Her mother sighed. "Well, earlier he was on Route 44 going through Tulsa. It'll probably be at least another day till he gets here."

Bethany nodded and her eyes drifted downward.

"He's coming as fast as he can, baby."

"I know," Bethany said. "Just bad timing, I guess, that he was out on the road when this happened."

"It'll be okay. Speaking of…last chance: you *sure* you'll be okay if I leave?"

"I am."

"Okay, baby. I love you."

"I love you too, Mom."

Bethany laid in a semi-upright position. Her wide-awake eyes stared out into the darkened ICU.

She thought about the tiny visitor from the night before and images of the gruesome event started to play on a loop in her head. Her hand hovered over the TV remote.

For the first time in several days, she wished she could turn on the television just to occupy her mind with something else. Perhaps there was a late night broadcast of the local news. Surely a rerun of *Seinfeld* would be on one of the networks.

Unfortunately, she knew the TV would be too disturbing for any of the other patients who were actually getting rest. But what if she muted the sound? She could find the subtitle options on the TV's remote and read along with the broadcast. All TVs came with

English subtitles now, right? She grabbed the remote and tried to find…

A disturbance in the quiet ICU ceased any ideas of watching television. Her attention turned towards the direction of the sound, which was that of somebody bumping into something metal, like a cart or a chair with metal legs. Bethany waited, expecting to hear a doctor or nurse's footsteps, but there was nothing.

She listened a bit longer, her ears acutely attuned to her environment: an overhead vent nearby slowly pushing air into the ICU, a ventilator humming along next to a sleeping patient, the gentle compression of a mattress due to a change in weight distribution.

Bethany spun her head. The little clown from before was straddling a male patient two beds away. He turned and smiled that evil, sadistic grin, the same one as the night before.

No, Bethany thought in terror.

The little clown raised a tiny hand; with the other, he held up a white plastic surgical glove. He slipped his hand into the glove, allowing it to *snap* closed around his wrist. Then he wiggled his fingers in a twisted 'jazz hands' gesture.

No!

In a single devastating motion, faster than Bethany knew was possible, the painted clown pulled out the patient's air tube and shoved his gloved hand into the man's mouth, deep into the throat, forcing his arm down until his elbow passed the lips.

"Help!" Bethany screamed. "He's here! He's here!"

The devil-clown reached into the patient's body a bit further, and then swiftly pulled out his arm. Bethany stopped screaming. The sound of the clown ripping his arm from the man's body was like that of pulling a package of innards out of an uncooked turkey.

She stared at the clown's hand and arm. Blood, flesh, stomach bile, gore…it all dripped from the clown's arm and onto the unmoving body.

The patient lay lifeless in the bed. The man's mouth remained open as more flesh, and a dark and viscous fluid spilled out over broken teeth and cracked lips.

Finally, Bethany remembered to breathe.

"Somebody help! He's killing him!"

Light again drowned the ICU in a whitish-yellow. Doctors and nurses raced to Bethany's bed. The brown-haired nurse that she had first seen upon waking appeared at the curtain.

"What do you need, dear?"

Bethany pointed in the direction of the slaughtered patient. "He killed him!"

The nurse looked over. She gasped and her head tilted in panic. "Oh my God…"

Before she could call for a code cart, other doctors and nurses had already arrived. Bethany leaned over and watched as they worked furiously to revive the patient. One doctor performed CPR, pressing madly into the man's chest at measured intervals.

"He's not gonna make it," another doctor said.

"Shut up, we've got this," a third doctor said.

The one who continued to perform chest compressions now had blood and pieces of entrails on his hands and white sleeves. "Come on," he grunted. "Don't do this…"

The brown-haired nurse ran around Bethany's bed and pulled the curtain to block her view.

"No!" Bethany said. "You have to find him!"

"Who?" the nurse asked.

"The little clown…thing! He's here!"

"Oh no…"

"Listen to me! I know you think I'm seeing things, but I'm not. He was here, he *was* here! He just reached into that man's throat and ripped his insides out!"

The nurse's eyes widened as if she, herself, was looking at a mad woman. "Okay…I think a sedative will do."

"No!" Bethany yelled. "I'm not seeing things! He's really here! You have to believe me!"

The nurse didn't respond, but scurried off only to return a minute later carrying a syringe.

"No…no…no," Bethany pleaded. She reached out and grabbed the nurse's shirt, pulling her close and gripping her arm.

"Okay, dear," the nurse said, "I need you to let go of me. Let go, please."

Bethany shook her head. "It's not what you think!"

"Please, I need you to let go." The nurse's voice was much louder now. "If you don't, this needle could end up hurting both of us."

Just then, another nurse and a doctor entered Bethany's space.

"Hold her down," the brown-haired nurse told them both.

The doctor and the other nurse grabbed Bethany's shoulders and forced her down into the bed. Bethany's grip on the nurse let go and the nurse injected the syringe into her IV bag.

Bethany continued to struggle until she felt herself lose both control and feeling of her hands and arms.

She blacked out.

"Oh my God!" Bethany's mother was appalled. Dr. Raimi had just explained that, similar to the night before, another patient in the ICU had an unfortunate accident.

This time, the patient had woken up during the night, became distraught and disoriented, and ultimately pulled out his own air tube. Doing this can tear the throat and cause massive bleeding, vomiting, and can lead to a patient choking and drowning in their own blood.

"Oh my God," her mother repeated. "This all happened last night?"

"I'm afraid so," Dr. Raimi said.

She turned to Bethany. "Oh…baby!"

"I'm fine, Mom. It's okay."

"I'm impressed by how well you're taking all this," the doctor said.

Bethany sighed. "Well, it's not every day you see someone die." There was a noticeable silence until Bethany added, "Well, maybe it is for me."

The doctor offered an expression of pity. "I'm going to make sure this doesn't happen again. I promise you, this doesn't happen very often, never mind twice in consecutive nights." Bethany nodded while the doctor continued. "I'm going to have a nurse stay in the ICU and keep you company tonight. She'll…"

Just then, the brown-haired nurse appeared.

"Speak of the devil," Dr. Raimi said. "Here she is now."

"How's my favorite patient this morning?"

Bethany forced a smile. "I'm good."

"Great! By the way, I feel terrible I haven't even given you my name yet."

"Well," Bethany said, "there hasn't been much time to talk."

The nurse laughed. "This is true. Well anyway, my name's Anna. Use the call button when you need it. If anyone other than me shows up, feel free to ask for me and they'll come get me."

"Sounds good," Bethany said.

"Speaking of good," Anna said, smiling, "Mom, Doctor...I think we've made some progress." She then turned to Bethany. "Isn't that right?"

Bethany smiled and nodded.

"What kind of progress?" Bethany's mother asked.

Anna prodded Bethany with her eyes.

"I know now that what I saw the last couple of nights is purely a figment of my imagination. It was probably just a dream."

The doctor's eyebrows rose. "That's very good to hear!"

"I know it's impossible for me to have seen what I think I saw," Bethany continued. "Now, I just have to tell myself it's not real any time I see something like that again."

Bethany's mother reached her arms around her daughter as tears rolled over her cheeks. "You're going to be just fine, honey. I promise. We'll get through this."

Bethany squeezed her mother back. "I know, Mom."

"Well howdy, everyone!"

The *zing* of a whistle and a squeaky horn caused them all to turn around. Bethany's body went cold and her heart filled with despair as she stared at the figure before her.

A man in full clown makeup and attire was blowing into a slide whistle, which rolled out of his mouth and extended three feet over her bed.

He then squeezed at a small bulb attached to a silver horn that let out several *honks*.

Bethany screamed.

At once, Dr. Raimi rushed the clown and pushed him out, and all the way through the doors of the ICU. Anna rested a hand on Bethany's head.

Bethany screamed again.

"I'm so sorry," Anna said. "We have a Care Clown that comes to the ICU every Wednesday. It's an attempt to cheer up people. This was highly inappropriate. Again, I'm so, so sorry."

Bethany stopped screaming, but she groped her mother's arms with a desperate intensity. Terror filled her eyes and she sobbed loudly, drooling onto her mother's clothing.

Her mother stared into Anna's eyes. "Please leave."

Anna nervously twisted her hands together. "Okay." She turned to leave and then spun around again. "I'm so sorry. I'm…" Then she left.

After a long afternoon, Bethany managed to calm down long enough to convince her mother to leave.

"You're out of your mind if you think I'm leaving," her mother said.

"Mom, it's fine. Seriously. Besides, Dad'll be home tonight and he'll be tired. It's better if you're home. Then you can drive him here and he doesn't have to be behind the wheel any longer than he has to."

"Your father can stay home by himself."

"Mom!"

Her mother sighed. "I know, I know…he really wants to see you."

"Well, there you go. He's *not* driving his rig here so, best if you're home. That way you can bring him here and he can even take a nap in the car on the way over. You can wake me up when you guys get back."

"Ha. Not a chance. You need rest."

"I got rest during the day."

"Rest? Is that what you call what you did today?"

Bethany's eyes drifted down, embarrassed. "I know…but it'll be fine. See?" She gestured toward Anna sitting at a desk in the middle of the ICU. "She'll be here all night."

Her mother sighed again. "Fine." She looked at her watch. "If I rush, I can probably get your father something to eat before he gets home."

"Perfect."

Her mother stared at her with eyes that looked as if they were staring at a helpless, newborn baby.

"Mom," Bethany said with a slight chuckle, "I'm fine."

"Okay. Be back in a while."

Actually, Bethany *had* gotten plenty of rest during the day. It was all part of a plan she was going to put into place that night. She was no good on both legs, that much was certain. But the patient next to her had a pair of crutches; they rested against the wall only a few feet away. Bethany would have to manage getting out of bed under her own strength, reach the crutches, and from there, make her best attempt to protect whichever patient appeared to be the most likely next victim.

As it were, there happened to be one patient who'd come in earlier in the day—a motorcycle accident had left his lower body shredded beyond belief. She'd overheard one doctor say it would be, "A miracle if he survived the night." Bethany wasn't a gambler, but she would have bet money on the man being the clown's next victim.

Luckily, Nurse Anna would be stationed at the desk in the ICU all night. When the clown finally showed up, there would be no way for her to refute Bethany's claims about the tiny murderer.

Anna sat with Bethany for a few hours, chatting into the night. They talked about Bethany's focus in college, where Anna had attended school, Bethany's post-college plans. Bethany was surprised that Anna wasn't much older than she, and had only graduated from nursing school a few years ago. She enjoyed Anna's company and wondered if they might stay friends even after her release from the hospital.

When it became very late, Anna reminded her it was quiet time in the ICU and they really shouldn't be talking as it could disturb the patients around them. Bethany understood and Anna walked back to the desk, swung open a laptop computer, and began typing.

Probably catching up on work, Bethany thought. *Wish I had something like that to keep me busy.* She looked over at a round wall clock across the room. It read 12:37 a.m. Her mom had left a long time ago. She assumed they would have been back by now.

She and Dad must be enjoying some alone time, she thought. Then she chased away an inappropriate image in her head.

A phone at the nurse's desk rang and Anna picked up the receiver. "Hello?"

Bethany waited as Anna paused, listening to the speaker on the other end of the line.

"Yes, they're parents of a patient in the ICU. What? Of course they can, that's absurd. Why can't they—fine. It's fine. I'll just…I'll be right there." She let out an exasperated sigh, pushed her chair away from the desk, and walked quietly over to Bethany. "I know you're not sleeping, so I figured I'd come and tell you. Our night security guard is giving your parents a hard time about coming back in. I told him it's fine, but…" She sighed again. "He's *very* by-the-book. Anyway, I'm going to go let them in. Only thing is, security is tighter at night so there's only one open entrance and it's at the north wing of the hospital, which is a few minutes' walk from here."

"Okay," Bethany said.

"I'm going to go get them, but it'll probably be about ten minutes. Are you good?"

Bethany nodded absently. She wanted to say no, that she wasn't good. Or that she needed Anna to stay. But for what reason? She couldn't tell Anna, "No, you can't go because there's an evil clown coming and I want you to see him!" Bethany had no cards to play at the moment. She was caught off guard and hadn't expected Anna to leave at any point during the night. She would be on her own. It was only for ten minutes, though, and maybe not even that long. What could possibly happen in such a small span of time?

Bethany watched Anna disappear through the main door of the ICU and she dropped her head, eyes staring forward at nothing.

Ten minutes, ten minutes. Only ten minutes.

The ICU was quiet, even quieter than before now that Bethany didn't have Anna's typing to keep her company. The dim light in the otherwise darkened room did nothing to make the place feel less creepy. Bethany started to count the minutes, hoping the activity would ease her own anxiety while she waited for Anna to return with her parents. She had counted two full minutes when a noise ripped her mind away from the exercise.

She twisted her neck, hoping to catch a glimpse of whatever had caused the sound. Then, in a moment of high alert, Bethany swept aside her bed sheets, pulled her damaged leg over the side of the mattress, swung over her good leg, and attempted to slide off the bed.

She managed to land and steady herself on her good leg. She then held onto whatever options were available—IV pole, computer-on-wheels, counter, monitor—as she hopped towards the other patient's crutches.

There was another noise, closer this time, and Bethany glanced at the motorcycle accident victim a few beds away. She grabbed the crutches, positioned one under each arm, and quickly scuttled around her neighbor's bed. When she made it around, she looked up again at the accident victim.

The clown was already straddling him.

"Get off of him," Bethany demanded.

The clown reached down at the patient's stitched-up wounds, and with one sharp, claw-like fingernail, plucked at one of the stitches. It came free with a *snip* sound. Bethany labored on the crutches as she approached the little clown.

"I'll yell so loud this place'll be swarming with staff. You'll never escape."

The clown feigned a nervous expression, his eyes wide and his tiny mouth forming 'O'. Then he laughed softly and plucked another stitch. Bethany hobbled even faster. She was about to reach the patient's bed when the clown pointed a claw-nailed finger at her. She stopped.

"Don't take another step," he said. His voice was grainy but high-pitched. "For if you do, I'll remove all his stitches with one swipe, and you'll be the one they see standing over him when they come to find out which patient is crashing."

Bethany bit at her lip while she contemplated her decision. He was right. He was just small enough to sneak away should anything get chaotic. Bethany, on the other hand, would never make it back to her bed before the first doctor or nurse rushed into the ICU, not on one good leg. They'd blame her. They'd see the dying patient, bleeding from his wounds, and they'd all point fingers at Bethany. After all, a patient had died each night she'd been in the ICU so far. From an outsider's perspective, it would make sense. Bethany stared into the clown's demon-like red eyes. She thought about how her mother and father had always taught her to do the right thing, to never back down from doing what she knew was right.

Screw it, she thought.

"Help me!" she yelled. "Help!" At the same time, she steadied herself on her good leg, grabbed hold of a single crutch with both hands, and swung it at the clown. A half-second before the crutch caught the clown in the head, his razor-sharp nails dug into the patient's abdomen and ripped out all his stitches as the clown tumbled away and off the bed.

"Help!" Bethany yelled again. The clown was on the floor, dazed and off-balance; Bethany raised the crutch over her head and brought it down with full force. She caught him on the top of the skull. She knew she hit him hard when she heard a dull grunt come from the tiny man.

Bethany squeezed her eyes closed and continued to strike at the clown. She thought about what she could have done to save the lives of the other patients if she'd only acted the same two nights earlier. Perhaps she could have saved one or even both of them. Then maybe the entire hospital, and her own mother, wouldn't think she was crazy. At one point, she raised the crutch but found she could no longer bring it down. Panicked, she opened her eyes.

There were doctors around, nurses, too. She looked around top see that an orderly had grabbed the crutch from her.

"Did you get him?" Bethany asked. "Did you see him? He was right here!"

She turned back to the crowd of doctors and saw a very large, male orderly rush at her. He wrapped his arms around her, lifted her off her feet and slammed her to the ground. The pain of her fractured leg crashing to the floor sent stars through her vision. She screamed and yelled to let her go, to find the small clown, but nobody would listen to her. Through her tears she saw gore and entrails on the floor. More blood and more parts of the patient's insides continued to fall and she could hear the heart monitor's one-note song playing the patient's final coda.

Pinned to the cold floor, Bethany looked past the rushing feet and legs of those trying to save the patient's life. Down the hall, she saw a tiny figure getting on an elevator. Bethany squinted to get a better look. As the elevator doors closed, the small figure turned around and Bethany saw the red eyes and curled lips of the clown.

Before she could do or say anything however, she yelped at the familiar pinch of a needle piercing her skin and tried to refocus her eyes. The little clown offered a wave of his hand, but Bethany never saw it as the sedative knocked her out.

A doctor with a tweed coat and freshly-pressed pants sat across from her. He'd told Bethany his name before, but she didn't care to remember it. She watched his pencil move across a small notebook. "Dude, you're not digital yet?" she'd asked him before, though she knew he was 'old school.' She'd remembered that much.

The window in her tiny room allowed a bit of moonlight to fall over part of her bed and a section of the floor. The doctor had paid a late visit. Rare, but not so much that it never happened. Bethany just preferred that he come earlier in the day. She'd much rather be getting ready for bed now that the sun was down.

The door to her room remained closed, just as it did during every session. An orderly stood outside until the doctor and Bethany were finished talking.

He finished making a few notes and asked, "So, what's your plan, Bethany?"

She stared at him intently, but not too much so that he would think she was trying to intimidate him. She knew it wouldn't work anyway, but she didn't want to be a bitch, either. Mostly, she attempted to appear pensive.

"I just want to get better," she said after a strategically timed and well-rehearsed sigh.

"That's good," he said. "We all want you to get better."

" 'We?' "

"Sure. Me, your parents, your doctors…we all want what's best for you."

"Why? So you can determine I'm competent and I can be sent to a real prison?"

"Do you think you belong in prison?"

Bethany laughed. "How am I supposed to answer that? I mean, really?"

"I just want to know how you feel, Bethany."

Her eyes found the ceiling and she betrayed her patience. "Feel about what, *Doctor*?" She said the word as if she was abusing it.

"About the patient that died in the ICU."

"You mean, did I kill him?"

The doctor didn't answer, but merely stared back. Bethany shook her head, frustrated.

"You know just as well as I do that even though I was there, not a single hair or drop of DNA or epithelial or any part of me was found on that patient. His blood wasn't even on me."

" 'Epithelial?' " the doctor asked with a smile. "Someone's been keeping up with her *CSI*."

Bethany ignored the joke. "I didn't kill anyone."

The doctor regrouped after his failed attempt. "That's true, there was physically no way you could have killed him, and your polygraph tests continue to come back negative. But you must have an idea of what happened."

She shook her head again. "You're amazing."

"Tell me."

Bethany looked straight into his eyes. "I believe the patient bled out due to complications with his injuries."

The doctor smiled. "Is that what you truly believe?"

Bethany nodded.

"Well, that's great," the doctor said. He flipped back a few pages in his notebook and slid a finger down a page until he found what he was looking for. "Unfortunately, Elizabeth told me just an hour ago that you were still hung up on this clown thing."

Her face dropped; she had now been betrayed twice this morning, once by herself and now once more by her only friend in the ward.

"Any idea why she'd say that?" the doctor asked.

Bethany stood up, walked over to the door, and banged on it. "We're done here," she said.

The door was unlocked a moment later and a tall, muscular man walked in. The doctor waved his hands in defeat. He reached down into the backpack sitting against his chair, filed away his pencil and notebook, and stood up to leave.

"Eventually," he said, "you're going to have to talk to me. Otherwise," he waved a hand around the room, "this is going to be home for the rest of your life."

"Aw, you mean no white picket fence?"

The doctor narrowed his eyes briefly and said, "Goodbye, Bethany." He left with the orderly and the door was closed. Bethany heard the lock engage and she knew she was finally alone for the night.

She moved over to the chair where the doctor was sitting, at the desk that displayed a few framed pictures. She held one photo of her and her parents at her high school graduation. Everybody was smiling.

Endless possibilities, she thought to herself. She'd never considered *this* possibility.

She heard voices on the other side of her door and she put the picture back down on the desk. She walked over to the door and pressed her face against the small, square window. She could see the psychiatrist talking with one of the doctors in the ward. Their voices were muffled, indiscernible, but she knew they were talking about her. She wondered what they were saying and if either of them thought she had a real shot at ever getting out of the ward. She knew she hadn't done herself many favors and figured she should start trying to win over—*Melbourne! His name's Dr. Melbourne!*—before he gave up on her.

The two doctors finally left, and Bethany remained with her face against the tempered glass. She stayed that way for a few minutes, lost in thought, lost in time…in memories she would never get to share with anyone ever again. She was about to lay down on her bed when she heard someone walking down the hall.

The person's feet sounded odd, not like shoes or sneakers, which were the usual footwear of the ward's staff. This person's feet seemed to *slap* against the tile floor, echoing sharply through the hall. Bethany could now see a shadow and her pulse quickened—it was a very short person.

Please, God, no…

The stranger continued to creep up the hall, and from her disadvantaged angle, Bethany could almost see the figure. She could see shadowed arms swinging freely, a head seemingly bobbing back and forth.

The silhouetted half-bald head was a dead giveaway.

No, it can't be.

The little clown was now in plain sight. There wasn't a doctor around, nor a nurse or an orderly. The clown strolled up to Bethany's door, looked up at the small window, and smiled malevolently.

Bethany's tears were the first she'd cried in months. Not since the night the third patient had died did she cry so hard. Even when her parents would visit, they were happy. They didn't cry because they didn't want Bethany to think her situation was forever. Therefore, Bethany didn't cry either.

Until now.

The small clown waved a white-gloved hand and walked across the hall. He stopped at room 104, which was directly across from Bethany's room. He jiggled the handle a bit, then the door gave way and he walked in. Just before he was inside, he turned back, winked at Bethany, and closed the door.

"No!" Bethany screamed and started pounding at her door. "Help! No!" She kicked her door hard several times and then stopped to hear if anyone was coming, but it seemed to her that this part of the ward was unsupervised at the moment.

Defeated, she sank down to the floor, her back to the door, and sobbed harder. There was nothing to be done. Nothing to do but wait for the screaming from across the hall to begin.

Bethany squeezed her eyes closed and gritted her teeth. She pounded a fist against the door again, slowly, methodically, hoping someone would hear her eventually and come see what all the noise was about.

Meanwhile, the screaming in room 104 had begun.

TO KILL A CLOWN

MICHAEL D. GRIFFITHS

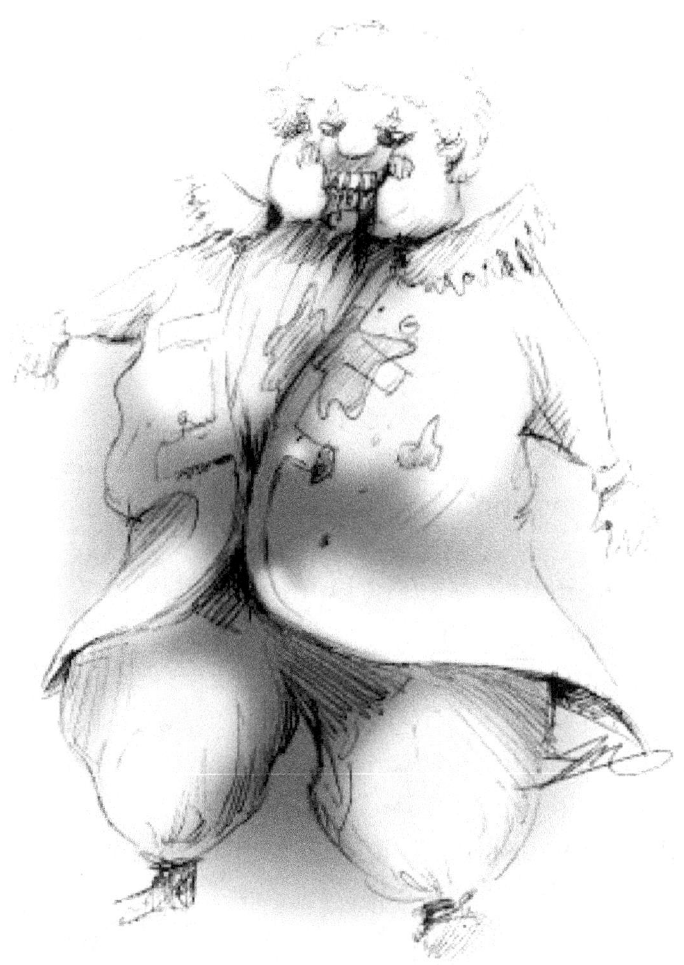

"How much cotton candy can one guy eat?" his wife asked. "I wanted him to share."

"Good luck with that one," Matt said. "If anything, he'll want a second one." As he spoke, he looked down at his young son. The cotton candy held the happy-eyed boy's natural tendency in check for the moment, but he knew his son's 'terrible twos' could erupt at any moment, which would require Matt to act quickly or lose his energy-filled son within the moving crowd.

After grabbing his son's small fingers, Matt helped guide the boy through the bright-colored masses. The sun warmed Matt's cheek as he took in the sweet smells of a dozen types of food. He wanted to sample them all, but knew he barely had enough money to warrant them even coming to the fair. Still, with a day like this blessing them on a Saturday, it would have been a crime to keep his son locked up inside.

Soon, the smells of the food began to overpower Matt's will and he stopped to look at the prices on the different display boards. He let go of his son's hand and counted his money. "A lot of this stuff is pretty expensive. I guess I'm going to get into the hot dog line," Matt said. Looking around, he saw his wife wasn't near him. She stood about twenty feet away watching a man blow glass.

Then it hit him like a bolt of lightning.

He couldn't see his son.

His eyes darted right and left, but still no sign of his son. His face felt flushed and he had a hard time drawing breath into his lungs. After another frantic search of the area, he ran to his wife.

"Sammy's missing," he said quickly.

"What!" she yelled, then joined him in scanning the crowd. "We have to find him right now!"

"Of course we do," Matt said. "But we can search faster if we split up. I'll go ahead and you backtrack. No matter what happens, meet me back in front of the hot dog stand in five minutes, okay?" When she didn't answer, he grabbed her arm. "Okay?"

She just nodded, but he could see that even while they talked her eyes searched for their missing son. He gave her a hug and a kiss. "We'll find him," he added and then rushed off.

Matt entered parts of the carnival they had yet to explore. He moved past the prize booths at a half jog. The carnies in this section were more suspect than at the front of the fair. Unshaved beards were topped by scowls, and tattoos and piercings covered much of their exposed flesh.

Any hope that his son might have stopped to admire a toy or an oversized stuffed animal proved short-lived and Matt hurried on. As if to match his mood, a dark cloud crossed the sun. He glanced up, surprised to see what could be rain-laden clouds where there had so recently been none. When he looked back, he thought he spied a figure covered with a chaotic mix of bright colors. He'd been looking for his son's red shirt, and there were large spans of reds that mixed with dark blues, yellows and whites.

It took Matt a second to realize it was a clown, for as soon as he had spotted the figure, the clown had already begun to disappear behind a shabby, off-white tent. He might have looked elsewhere if he hadn't heard a faint cry coming from the region of the retreating clown.

It was hard to tell, but the sound reminded Matt of one of his son's squeals. *It's probably some stupid clown thing*, he thought, but went off in that direction anyway.

Upon reaching the far side of the grimy tent, Matt saw no sign of the clown. He was about to turn around when he heard another whimper. He'd reached the far side of the carnival; nothing was beyond this area save a cluster of mismatched vehicles.

Against his better judgment, Matt decided to peek into the tent. He could find no opening on the side he was on, which made the sudden disappearance of the clown even stranger.

He was about to leave when he spotted the remains of a cotton candy stick peeking out from under the bottom lip of the tent. It was the same color as the one his son had been eating. Matt reached down and picked it up. As he did so, it caught on the tent and lifted up the edge. He saw that the tent sides were quite loose and were able to rise a long way off the ground.

"Screw it," he said in a low voice, then dropped onto his hands and knees near the edge of the tent. With his left hand, Matt lifted the edge of the tent and peered into the dark interior.

As soon as he lifted the material, he heard a sound that remained hard to place—a sort of tearing. This was quickly followed by a burst of giggles that for some reason hit a core within his psyche that sent chills up his spine.

It was like the laughter of a madman in a psych ward peeling away his own flesh, or a demented child delighting in the suffering of a helpless animal.

Thoughts of his own safety were pushed aside. If there was even a small chance that those horrid sounds could have something to do with his son's disappearance, Matt needed to get into that room at once.

He made it under the tent flap without trouble, but found himself trapped between the legs of a folding table. He tried to hurry ahead, but saw the way blocked by a colorful bulk of loose clothes that clung to a fat form, like someone had tried to slip a loose dress over the legs of an elephant. Beyond the legs, Matt heard a muffled voice struggling to say something, but even with the mouth obstructed he thought he heard the voice say, "Dah!"

It was his son. The clown had his son!

He pushed against the wide, concealed legs and his hand slipped off the polyester as the form retreated. He hadn't expected it to give way so suddenly and he fell forward on his hands and knees.

The insane giggle sounded from above, but before he could look into the face of the clown-faced villain, something hard and unforgiving crashed down onto the back of his head. He struggled to stay conscious, but the last thing he remembered was falling face first onto the figure's big red floppy shoes.

When he awoke, pain ruled him. His forehead hurt so bad it remained hard to think. He tasted blood and felt like he'd been chewing on copper. Confusion filled him for a moment, but then his situation came back to him in waves. He shook his head to clear it a few times. But where some people might have felt fear, rage took over Matt and he struggled to get up only to find himself bound.

"Give me a break…" he said aloud when he saw that different-colored balloons were being used to tie him to a strong wooden chair. He figured he could break through them easily, but instead found that that they didn't budge. There were so many on him that his arms and legs couldn't move at all. He let loose a string of curses until he realized he should try to stay silent until he could figure out what to do next.

The first step was to take in where he was.

He might have been in the same tent he had tried to sneak into before. All around him were piles of stuffed animals and other toys. Filled balloons bounced on the floor as well as the roof of the tent. Cakes and candies sat in a huge mess on one table, but a table on the opposite side of the room was covered with items far more sinister: knives of every imaginable sort mixed with axes and hatchets. Other items like crowbars looked marred with rust or at least Matt hoped it was rust. Looking closer, he saw that many of the blades were covered with the same coating as well.

He struggled anew with the same results. He found it strange that he hadn't been gagged and considered screaming, but with the noise of the carnival outside the tent, he figured it would be useless. He decided to keep the idea in reserve; better to try and escape before the clown or whoever had knocked him out and bound him, realized he was awake.

The he heard something. Usually it was a noise that brought a smile to his face, but this time his delighted son's shriek of happiness only brought fear to Matt's heart.

Sammy was inside of the tent with him.

He hadn't noticed his son before; Sammy was hiding behind a giant stack of stuffed animals, but there was no mistaking the sounds of his son.

"Sammy," Matt whispered. "You okay? Come here, Sammy."

His son's smiling blonde head peeked over a giant bear in a clown suit. He held up a toy fire engine, covered with foolish plastic clowns, like a director showing off his Oscar.

"What do you have there, son? Show it to Daddy."

Sammy stood up, looking as cute as ever. His toddler waddle would have been a joy to see under different circumstances, but now it only reminded Matt of the hopeless situation they were both in.

But some things didn't change no matter what the situation, and Sammy tossed the fire engine right onto Matt's nuts. "It figures," Matt said with a wince. "Thanks, son."

Then Matt had to focus. He knew he might just have seconds before the clown returned. "Sammy, can you find Mommy? Go get Mommy."

Sammy looked around the tent, like he would have liked to help, but with no mother in sight, he left the engine on his father's lap and waddled over to a rocket ship that also appeared to be manned by clowns.

Matt struggled again to get free, but it was no use. It pained him that something as silly as balloons might end up spelling the doom for both him and his son. He wanted to try and have Sammy find him a knife, but didn't want the boy to get hurt doing so.

"Who am I kidding? You aren't really at the 'go-fetch-me-a-knife' stage yet, huh, buddy?" A tear slowly slipped down his face when his son looked up at him. "I love you, buddy. I'm sorry. I'm so sorry."

Matt heard something moving behind him and the hairs on the back of his neck started to rise. It was also at this moment that he noticed one of the top rungs on the fire engine toy was broken.

Normally, such a thing would have worried him if it was within the vicinity of his boy, but this time it filled him with hope.

If I can get that sharp edge under one of these balloons, he thought.

He started to try at once. Shifting his thighs brought the top of the ladder close to a balloon, but one of the wrong ones. It was mid-forearm instead of near his wrist.

Screw it, he thought. *Better than nothing.*

He began to move his leg so the ladder would cut into the pink balloon wrapped around his arm.

He was surprised how quickly it worked. Once a cut was made the tightness of the balloon caused it to snap on its own.

More clanking sounds came from behind. Then there was the sound of a hundred marbles bouncing off a table.

His son looked up from his playing.

"Stay here, buddy. Stay with Daddy."

With a smile, Sammy went back to the toy.

Matt then maneuvered the ladder under the balloon holding his wrist down. It was at a more difficult angle, but he got it to cut the balloon. Again it fell away with a loud snap. He was lining it up to cut the second balloon near his wrist when a loud horn honked right behind him.

He cried out despite himself.

A second later, a horrid-colored face full of dripping makeup stared at him from just inches away. Eyes filled with a burning madness were surrounded by white and black layers of face paint. Red lips formed a smile that clashed with the man's real expression. The rest of the outfit was colorful and extreme, but ratty, as though it had been worn for years without repair. The clown also stank, and Matt wondered if the foul costume was ever taken off.

"Naught-naughty. I think you've had enough play time with that toy for now," the clown said in an annoying child's voice. He grabbed the toy from Matt and flung it across the tent.

"But we're going to have a lot more fun, right, Timmy?" The clown said to Sammy.

Sammy looked like he wasn't sure whether he should laugh at the funny face or break into tears. Instead, he looked at his father.

"Go find Mommy," Matt begged. "Please son, run. Run away right now!"

"No-no! We need to *play*!" the clown yelled before striking Matt in the face with something that looked like an old sock. Matt gasped from the blow, for the sock felt like it was stuffed with needles and thorns. Matt tasted blood again. Rage won out over his fear once more. He glared at the clown angrily.

"Oh-oh. Daddy doesn't like playing so much. We'll have to think of a new game then. Would you like me to play with you first or would you rather see how I'll be playing with Timmy?"

"Let me loose and we'll really play, you insane coward," Matt said through clenched teeth.

"So you aren't afraid of me," the clown said in his high-pitched voice. "But I know what will make you afraid, very afraid. Come here, little Timmy."

"No, Sammy, stay away from him. Get out of here!"

Instead of going toward the old toys that lay on the flattened and yellow grass that made up the ground, the tattered-suit clown walked toward the table full of rusty tools and blades. "I have all sorts of fun toys, Timmy. I bet you've never played with some of these before."

"You sick bastard," Matt snarled as he struggled to break his arm free. With two of the balloons gone, he was able to lift his arm about half an inch, but could only hold it there for a few seconds. He tried again with similar results. Looking over at the table, he saw the clown picking through his tools while he sung disturbing nursery rhymes.

"Jack and Jill went up the hill to fetch a pail of blood. But the well was dry so he stabbed her eye and Jack ran down and her body came tumbling after."

Matt lifted his arm again, and this time tried to pull it out from under the balloons. They caught and tore at his skin, but he ignored the pain. Clenching his teeth, he kept trying. Glancing back again, he saw the clown still searching for the proper tool.

He jerked when his son's body collided into his legs.

Sammy was proudly holding up a new toy puppy that attempted to bark, but its low batteries just left it sounding like something slowly dying underwater. "Doggie."

"Good boy," Matt whispered. "Go show it to Mommy. Go find Mommy."

"Mum," Sammy said while he looked around the tent.

Matt was already working on getting free again. Maybe it was his son's proximity that fueled his efforts, but with a final, massive pull, he jerked his right arm free.

"Hey now, that's not part of the rules!" the clown yelled in his helium voice as he rushed over.

Matt tried to urge his son toward the tent flap. "Go find Mommy, honey, please."

"He's gong to play with *me*!" the clown yelled as he pushed Sammy away from Matt.

Sammy tumbled to the ground and began to cry at once. Long wails filled the tent, but still no one came to their aid.

"All right, Chuckles, that's it!" Matt shouted and clawed at the clown's face. The madman pulled back, but Matt's hand grasped his nose. It was on some sort of rubber band which stretched away from the clown's head until it slipped out of Matt's fingers, only to return to smack the clown in the face.

"Ouch, that hurt!" The clown yelled while clutching his face. Then he went on in an annoying sing-song voice, "But I can hurt, too." A blood-stained knife flashing overhead, the mad clown stabbed Matt in the upper right shoulder. He leaned over Matt, the knife keeping Matt in place. "You want your arm free so bad, let's just free it from… your… body!"

The clown clutched at Matt's free arm as he withdrew the knife and raised it high again. "It's been a while since I severed an adult's arm, but I'm sure it's the same as the little ones." He giggled. "It'll just take a few more hacks."

Still trapped in the chair, Matt wasn't sure what to do, but knew he had less than a second to decide before the knife pierced his flesh. He thought of what would happen to his son if he failed in this fight, and a red haze washed over him. His rage took control, blocking out everything else in a red haze.

As the knife blade came down, and the clown giggled manically, Matt jerked forward, smashing his forehead into the clown's nose as the madman leaned forward to stab him. The blow shattered the clown's nose with an explosion of blood. "There you go, Chuckles, more face paint, free of charge," Matt hissed.

The clown lowered the knife and his free hand covered his bleeding nose, but then he screamed and lifted the knife anew. "I'm not Chuckles. My name is Giggles."

"Big fucking difference!" Matt shouted, his free hand darting forward like the fangs of a striking snake, his fingers straight. Matt tried to blind the clown, but only managed a glancing blow. Still, it was enough to send Giggles stumbling backwards, crying like a dropped baby as he felt his wounded eye with his free hand. "My eye, my eye! I don't want to wear an eye patch. I don't want to be a pirate clown." He kept backpedaling away from Matt until his legs hit Sammy, where the boy still sat crying. With cart-wheeling arms, Giggles tripped over Sammy and fell backwards. His head hit the seat of a tricycle, and he let out a gasp, then went still.

Sammy's tears stopped as he gazed over at the fallen clown. He stood up on shaky legs, then bent down and picked up the dirty knife.

"Good boy, Sammy. Bring that to Daddy."

Sammy looked uncertain.

"Please bring that to Daddy."

Sammy took a few steps closer, but as he did, Giggles started to groan.

"Damn it, he's not dead. Sammy, I need you to bring me that knife."

With a smile, Sammy tottered over and held up the knife to his father. Matt grabbed it from Sammy's little fingers just as the clown started to live up to his name and began giggling.

It took Matt only seconds to cut his left arm free. He freed his right leg and was working on his left when something crashed down on his head. He saw white stars and had to fight to remain conscious. It hurt worse than anything he could remember.

"How do you like it?" Giggles asked, laughing manically again.

Looking up, Matt saw he'd been hit with a brightly-colored wooden box with pictures of dancing clowns painted on the side. Giggles lifted the box again and Matt knew he might not survive another blow.

This time Giggles proved smart enough to stay clear of Matt's stabbing range, so instead Matt used his free leg to topple the chair over backwards.

"I'll just break your legs then," Giggles snickered.

Matt said nothing, only growled, as his free foot kicked Giggles in the groin. The clown stumbled back with a loud gasp, his eyes as big as dinner plates.

"I'll kill your son for that," Giggles squeaked when he'd caught his breath again.

But Matt had already begun sawing at the last of the balloons binding him to the chair, though the awkward angle made cutting the last balloons more difficult.

Giggles had enough time to snatch up Sammy before Matt could get free and make it to his feet.

"I have your son," the clown giggled.

"And I have your knife."

The moment stretched while they stood facing each other. In the distance, Matt heard his wife calling his and Sammy's names.

"Mommy," Sammy said and tried to wiggle free of the clown.

Giggles hadn't been expecting it and his bloody hands couldn't maintain his grip on the squirming child.

Sammy fell to the ground.

Giggles looked at the boy and then his wide eyes shifted back to Matt.

"Laugh this off, funny man," Matt said as he fenced forward with the knife and stabbed Giggles in the throat. The clown clutched at his neck before stumbling backwards and falling over the toys.

Matt hurried to pick up his son while he pointed the bloody knife at the clown. "You should be happy, dumb ass. I gave your face an extra grin." He had, too. The knife had sliced the throat in a way that it looked like a smiling face had been carved into the clown's neck.

Never taking his eyes off the clown, Matt moved to the closest tent wall. He stabbed the knife through the material and cut down. As soon as he had created an opening, he called out his wife's name as loud as he could. She appeared at the cut tent opening seconds later.

"Oh my God! Matt!"

He passed Sammy through the hole. "Just take him and…"

Suddenly, thick fingered, rubbery hands grabbed Matt's neck from behind and pulled him back into the tent. The clown kept trying to giggle, but it came out sounding like a man dying from lung cancer. Matt was being dragged back toward the table piled his with weapons, and the suddenness of the attack had caused him to drop the knife.

"Son of a…" he growled and then elbowed the clown in the gut. Spinning, he said, "Sometimes the old fashion ways work the best." He punched the clown in the face and Giggles went toppling back into the table, knives and other items of torture falling to the ground in a clang of metal.

Giggles stood back up with a whine and then fell face first onto the ground. Matt quickly found the source of the clowns collapse, for half a dozen blades protruded from Giggle's back.

"Finally," he said, wiping his forearm across his wet forehead.

When he looked back toward the hole in the tent, he was surprised to see his wife climbing through.

He moved forward. "No, get him out of here. Sammy doesn't need to see any more of this."

But then he saw the look of terror on her face and heard the chilling sound of more laughter. In the gloom of the tent, he could just make out the rows of brightly-colored outfits, while behind him, the tent flaps opened on all sides and a horde of clowns riding silly bicycles came into the tent.

There were at least twenty of them.

THE LEGACY OF JO-JO THE CLOWN

TONY GARCIA

Prologue

*D*rip...*drip*...*drip*.

Crimson rubies fell from his fingers only to pool at his feet. Poetry in slow-motion. Divinity. Transfixed, he watched the flow as it left her body, glistening in the moonlight. Within the dark pool a young girl lay twisted, contorted, head pointed as if facing the sky, one arm poised above her head, the other gracefully behind her, one leg bent as if at any moment she would take flight. He had created the perfect ballerina.

She was beautiful.

She would never be more beautiful than she was right now. Sounds erupted all around him, shouting, crying, screaming, and music to accompany his bloody dancer. No, he reflected, now it was perfect.

Hands dragged at him, fists hammered at him, knives stabbed his flesh; none of it mattered. He was lifted above them, exalted beneath the glowing moon as she stared down upon him, her spotlight—his center act.

Something tightened against his throat, a medal for his artistry no doubt, constricting, choking. Art was pain, life was pain, and pain was art. His feet dangled beneath him as the warm breeze gently swayed his body like a baby in a basinet.

They were all around him, faces, leering, shouting, frothing, critics, fans—the jealousy was empowering. Swinging to and fro, his eyes never lost focus on his masterpiece until the moon finally called him home and blackness swallowed him whole.

This performance would be his legacy.

Jeff and Russell staggered and belched their way down *Circus Circus Drive*, the warm bouquet of the Las Vegas sewer slapping them in the face with every breeze. Laughing and swinging a near empty bottle of whiskey, they made damn sure to represent every bad quality associated with tourists.

At first glance they either looked like a couple of guys who would never hang out together or like best friends. Jeff was tall and gangly while Russell was short and stocky. Even their clothes were direct contrasts.

Russell, with his dark beady eyes and brown hair pulled back in a short ponytail, wore a plain black t-shirt and blue jeans; the exact same thing he wore every day of the week. When asked he would say, "Hey, Einstein and Goldblum had a bunch of the same shirts and pants so that way they never had to waste time deciding on an outfit, so if two freakin' geniuses like them can do it, so can I!"

Not that anyone ever suspected Russell of being a genius, as Jeff so often liked to point out. Jeff had a mop of red curly hair framing his freckled face; he always wore loose, baggy polo shirts and cargo pants that looked two sizes too big, and as if they'd just been pulled from the laundry pile off his floor, which was often very true.

"Where the hell is this place?" Jeff asked for the thirtieth time in half as many minutes.

"I told you. The directions said it's just off *Circus Circus Drive* near the intersection of *Industrial Road*." Jeff pointed at the street sign directly above Russell's head. "Now all we have to do is take a left and follow it to the end."

"The chicks better be as hot as...hey! What the fuck?" Jeff yelled, jumping back as a large splash of dirty water exploded in front of him. The voice that followed wheezed with laughter and greeted them from overhead.

"Sorry, boys, ah didn't see you there!"

Slowly, they gazed upward, focusing blurry eyes on the source of the interruption. An old man, easily in his late seventies, wearing grubby coveralls and clutching a bucket and a squeegee, met their gaze from the climbing scaffold just over their heads.

"What the fuck is wrong with you, you crazy old bastard?" Russell was never known for his tact.

"Ah said I was sorry, boy," the old man retorted with no small amount of feigned hurt in his voice. "Ah just didn't see you two walkin' whiles I dumped mah bucket is all. No reason to get yer panties in a bunch."

Jeff jumped in, hoping to stop Russell from making things worse "He's fine. He just gets this way when strangers throw stuff at him. Happens all the time." He flashed his best friendly smile and hoped he didn't look as retarded as he felt.

"Well, you'd think I ran over his dog by the look on his sour mug!"

"No, that's normal too...um...so what *are* you doing up there? Uh..."

"Name's Clancy."

"Okay...Clancy. What are you doing with a bucket this late at night?"

Waiving upwards with his squeegee, Clancy said, "Ah'm cleanin' the clown, boy. What the hell does it look like ah'm doin'?"

Looking up, the two men noticed the giant clown marquee behind Clancy.

Looming high above them, one flickering neon hand seemed to point directly at them, while in the other hand the clown was brandishing a red neon pinwheel, as if ready to strike. Yellow, triangular eyes and a wide, gaping red smile glowed in the dark, seeming to stare right at them, despite the involuntary shudder both men experienced. It must be the booze playing tricks, they figured. Neither Jeff nor Russell could peal their eyes away from the garish display. There was nothing happy or funny about the clown, at all, and even its smile was disturbing and cast chills over them.

"That is the creepiest clown I've ever seen," Jeff mumbled, and Russell nodded silent agreement, which he punctuated by a hefty swig of whiskey.

"I doubt it," Clancy muttered under his breath.

"What was that?" Russell asked, his eyes still locked on the marquee in macabre fascination.

"Hmm? Oh, nothin'. You boys look like you ain't never seen a clown before!" Clancy's laugh was creepy enough to break the spell, and now all focus was on the old man as he spoke. "Hell, ah bet you don't even know the legend behind old Jo-Jo here, do you?" He jerked his thumb backwards, gesturing to the clown, but dumb shrugs were his only response. Sighing, he pulled a lever, lowering the scaffolding just enough to place him at eye level with Jeff and Russell. "You see, it goes like this..."

As the two men stared on, between swallows of their whiskey, Clancy weaved a tale about how *Circus Circus* was haunted and had been since it was built in 1968, but the land had been the stomping grounds of a long dead ghost since the 1930s.

According to Clancy, there was a serial killer responsible for dozens of bizarre murders during what he referred to as the *Dust Bowl Days*, and with as much concentration as the two slowly sobering drunks could muster, he held Russell and Jeff in thrall the entire time he spoke.

The killer—according to rumors and "*I shit you not*" firsthand witnesses, and even more secondhand accounts from people Clancy had met in his decades of life right here near this very spot—had traveled with a carnival dressed as a clown, and in almost every town the carnival stopped in, he left a victim brutally mangled in his wake—most often a young woman, but occasionally a man, or animal, but never a child for some unknown reason.

Surely the townsfolk blamed the carnies, but by the time the body was found the troupe was long gone and through some weird twist of fate never returned to that town. Clancy explained that some folk believed the killer was making some kind of weird artistic statement with the bodies, but most just knew it was the work of one sick sonofabitch.

Supposedly, some townsfolk finally caught the clown with one of the victims—his last victim...in this life anyway—and they proceeded to enact some quick *mob justice*. He was beat, stabbed, and finally hanged by the neck until dead. Some tell of how he just smiled through the whole thing, like nothing could hurt him, like none of it was real, like he wasn't altogether human. Others hear tell that a strange wind picked up as the last breath left his body, and it grew so strong they were forced indoors, leaving his body swaying in the desert gusts for days.

When the breeze finally died away and they came out to get rid of the corpse, all they found was the empty hangman's noose, still swinging to and fro. Some of them same folks claim they heard a sick laugh that sounded like it came from the very depths of Hell. No one story truly neither confirmed nor debunked any of the other tales, but one thing was for certain, Jo-Jo the Killer Clown was one scary bastard, dead or alive.

Time went by, and like most things, the story of Jo-Jo turned into a distant memory. But like most horrific tales, eventually, he was seen as just another boogeyman to frighten children into behaving.

Decades passed, people moved on, and the tale of the serial-killing clown they called Jo-Jo died away on the desert wind. In fact, no one gave it a second thought until they built the casino in the very spot he was killed.

Now, they didn't build the casino knowingly on top of a grisly murder site, or a supposed ghost haunt. In fact, no one even knew about the old story until after the grand opening...and that was when the weirdness started.

Nothing major at first: a breeze on a still night would blow out a candle, lights would flicker, a few unexplained chills, knocked over glasses, and the like. It was stuff so mild that the workers even started joking about the place being haunted by a friendly ghost. This apparently pissed off the ghostly specter something fierce.

One thing people forget about clowns is that the creepy bastards hate it when you make fun of them.

Small occurrences went on for a few years, but then, when everyone was so comfortable and used to the 'happy poltergeist' in their hotel—some said it was quaint even—it all stopped. Not gradual like, though, but all at once.

The ghost was gone and it stayed away for nearly five years. It was on the celebration of the tenth anniversary they found her. Nearly every bone in her body was broken and smashed, hanging like a limp rag doll from the central chandelier.

Her bloody legs were curled around a chandelier bar, the bones sticking through parts of her skin, and one arm was wrapped on another bar. She looked like one of those trapeze artists from the circus.

Some say she had a smile painted on her face...in her own blood.

Not a single person saw anything, no evidence of how she got up there, no fingerprints left behind, no motive, nothing. And to top it all off, nobody even knew who she was. As the investigation went on, the police figured out she was just a tourist traveling through town, and eventually, with no leads, no identification on her, no way of knowing who or where her kin were, and nothing else to go on, they closed the case as 'unsolved' and everyone moved on with their lives.

Rumors popped up about ghosts, and shortly afterwards, and once it started, it spread like wildfire. Pretty soon the idea for a 'great commercial stunt' was hatched, and they brought in so-called specialists to purify the casino, hold séances, and all kinds of nonsense that luckily was easy to find in Vegas.

As a bonus, the television people sent camera crews like a bunch of maggots. No one turned up anything, and since they couldn't prove or disprove anything, the 'experts' declared the casino was free and clear of evil spirits.

The newspapers ate it up, a real 'common interest' tale worth spewing all over the people so they'd buy some more crap they didn't need!

What didn't make the press however, was that three of the spiritualists had died in the casino under less than normal conditions...all unexplained like the first death...all covered up as bizarre suicides.

Anything else would be bad press, so why not capitalize on a few mysterious deaths for the sake of ratings? One was found drowned head first in the toilet, another with a smile carved from her throat to her ears, still clutching the bloody knife, and a third blew his brains out. The weird part on the last one was they found the gun in his hand, but they never found a bullet.

After the deaths the inspections stopped and the spiritualists stopped coming, and things slowly went back to mostly normal.

Since the incidents and just on the sake of being prudent, the staff made a point of never making a joke about the ghost, and some would even drink a toast to his spirit, and others, more sane folk that is, moved on to other employment.

Years passed quietly and they realized that the deaths had suddenly stopped, and for a long time there had been no weird activity at all. Old Jo-Jo had scared them all so badly that many of them didn't know what to do or how to act—after all, he might still be there, or if he was gone, he could still come back at any time.

Upon finishing the story, Clancy looked up at the sky and back to the boys and then down the street with a glassy-eyed thousand-yard stare.

"When?" Russell prodded after several awkward, but silent moments.

"When what?" Clancy quirked a brow.

"When did the deaths stop?"

"Wha...oh yeah, that was weird, too. Must've been the early seventies and then nothing till about five years ago." Clancy rubbed his chin, stared up at the sky, then back at the young men, and put his thumbs in his pockets.

"And then?" Russell blurted.

"Then what?" Clancy stared back.

"You said more people died about ten years ago! Why? What happened?"

"Oh, that. Well, not much to tell really. A few idjits from one of them ghost hunting programs came poking around and one of 'em fell out a window and died. They said it was an accident, but I figure it was 'cause they was askin' questions and it bein' the anniversary and all..."

"Anniversary of what?" Jeff held Russell back as he seemed about ready to lunge on top of the scaffolding and beat the story out of poor old Clancy.

"Damn boy, weren't you listenin'? It was the anniversary of the first killin' here." Clancy punctuated his question with an evil disapproving *you're a dumbass* glare.

Jeff stepped in front of Russell with a hand wave and a look that told Russell to back off and let him handle it. "Clancy, why did the killings stop? Did the ghost get his fill of revenge and then move on?"

"Why?"

"There has to be a reason why!" Russell ignored Jeff's silent protests. "I mean, a pissed-off ghost wouldn't kill a bunch of maids and frauds and then just vanish," Russell explained. "Did Jo-Jo kill everyone who mocked him like a tantrum? Did he just get bored? Was he exorcised? What caused it all to just stop?"

Clancy stared long and hard at Russell, then with another brief upward glance he rubbed his stubble chin and shrugged. "Well, there were rumors, but nothing was ever proven, just mostly guesses is all. Some figured he did just what you said. He got his revenge and moved on...but that don't account for all of it. There's still some unexplained things goin' on here, and some say...well, some say ol' Jo-Jo ain't done; he just likes to pick his victims from those that won't be missed is all."

"Those that won't be missed?" Russell asked, swallowing the knot in his throat.

"Yeah, you know, like someone that no one around these parts would hardly notice, or give two shits about when they was gone."

"Like who?"

"Like migrant workers, hoodoo voodoo types, homeless peo-ple, and... tourists." Clancy nodded, as if a heavy load had just been lifted from his shoulders. With a shrug he reached down to reclaim his bucket. "Well, boys, I got work to do and need to refill my bucket. So, if you'll excuse me."

He dropped down and walked away towards *Circus Circus* with a squeegee over his shoulder and whistling a low tune.

Stunned silence hung almost tangible in the air around Russell and Jeff for several minutes, then Jeff slowly got hold of himself and asked, "What the hell was that?"

"How the hell should I know? He's probably just a crazy old bastard with a screwed-up sense of humor, who's getting his rocks off scaring stupid tourists." Russell flipped the bird at the old man's back.

"Not psycho Clancy's story! What's...*that*?" Jeff pointed up and behind Russell, whose eyes slowly followed Jeff's shaking hand aimed up at the fluorescent demon clown. Despite himself, Russell flinched just enough to send Jeff doubling over in laughter and nearly falling over onto his face.

Above them loomed the marquee with its garish grin, but nothing had changed.

"You should have seen your face!" Jeff screamed between fits of laughter. "You nearly pissed your pants!"

"Very funny, asshole."

Suddenly, a large shadow overcame them, surrounding them and blotting out the lights of Vegas; it wasn't as if the lights had gone out like in a power outage, but an all encompassing darkness that swallowed light and color completely.

Standing on an unseen surface that shifted with every movement, Russell groped in the dark for something to hold on to, something to guide him, anything.

"Hey!" Jeff yelled.

But he only managed to punch Jeff in the nose. Nervous laughter filled the air momentarily, disguising their panic. At least each man knew the other was there and experiencing the same thing—the moment was short-lived.

Explosions of light began attacking them from all sides and above.

Pop! Sizzle! One after the other, bright white circles erupted and danced all around them, serenaded by the most hideous, screeching cackle ever imagined. Yellow lights flared and red fireworks burst in the darkness above, casting a hellish distortion reflected upon the ground. Somewhere, deep in the heart of chaos, music came: whining, tinny, scratching whispers of a dying phonograph.

Duhduh-Duh-Duhduh-Duh-Duh-Duh-Duh! An out of tune trumpet howled over a mix-match of drums and other less identifiable instruments, all fumbling their way into a warped carnival tune.

It just played on, never reaching an ending, never finding a beginning, it simply...was. In sync with the sound, swirling madness within the darkness began to take shape: a tent here, a pole there, leering faces from painted signs, swinging lanterns on poles, a ticket booth, a popcorn stand, and finally a hawker's stage right in front of a giant gray tent veined with red and black, looking all the while like diseased flesh.

The entire scene was lined from every pole, stake and seam, by flashing red lights, while shadows danced with the swinging gas lanterns. The overwhelmed senses of the two men, assaulted from every direction, threatened to leave them completely...yet all of this paled in comparison to the sight unfolding on center stage.

Standing nearly seven feet tall and more than half as wide, the clown stared down at them with blazing yellow eyes. The piercing, evil eyes belonged to a grotesquely fat head, crowned by a tangled mass of red and green hair that moved almost as if it was alive. Finishing the painting was his face: sweaty, greasy, and caked with white powder make-up; heavy black spikes were painted across each eye. A hideous crimson smile nearly split the face, displaying two rows of sharpened teeth.

"Step right up, folks!" A sound like fingernails being dragged across a chalkboard shattered the carnival music, and in its place was that voice. A voice comprising the worst elements of a butchered Vincent Price impersonator, one of the Beatles, and a mouthful of gravel all rolled into one.

"A show... to astound... and terrify..." The words came slow and deliberate "Amaze and mystify..." It made the two men's flesh crawl. "You'll laugh and you'll cry..." A voice only a nightmare could make "You'll kiss your soul goodbye." The demonic clown finished his introduction with a flourishing bow over his great stomach, causing all manner of objects to fall from within his overcoat: coins, a spool of thread, throwing knives, bowling pins, and a bloody rubber chicken became scattered across the stage, some rolling to the ground only to vanish within the blackness. With surprising speed and something almost resembling grace, he sprang from the stage to land directly in front of Russell and Jeff, who were both frozen in place, and wishing they could just wake up from whatever drunk blackout they were experiencing...together...at the same time.

"Tickets...tickets...tickets..." The clown held out a pale white fist the size of a bear paw. "What? No tickets?! How can you come... to a carnival... and expect to go on a ride... without a ticket? You can't...be serious! This is precisely the problem... with people these days! Everyone's a freeloader!"

Standing with hands on hips, he agitatedly tapped an enormous red shoe in mock indignation, then leaned forward, glaring at each young man in turn, as if sizing them up for worth or contemplating a family recipe.

Repugnant would be a compliment to the stench the clown emitted, and not just from the foulness that was his mouth, but from all about him came the scent of rot, decay, stale popcorn, urine, and cotton candy. "Ah... hmmm... the show must go on." With a sudden theatrical flourish of his massive arm and jiggle of bulbous gut, he proclaimed, "Ah, well, come one, come all...even you two deadbeats!" Spinning abruptly away from the two men, his shredded and stained trenchcoat flew behind him like tattered bat wings. Beneath the dated military jacket was an equally ripped t-shirt, and oversized, tacky black and gold striped pants that were tucked into huge crimson boots. "Grab a seat... the ride's about to start!"

Then, as abruptly as he appeared, the clown was gone, leaving behind only horrendous laughter that faded away to nothing. The carnival tents began melting away to be replaced by rusted metal tracks leading straight up, high above into absolute darkness. It was further than the two men's eyes could see.

Jeff and Russell suddenly realized in stunned silence that they were seated in an old roller coaster car, which was jerkily ascending the tracks.

THUNK – CLAK – THUNK! Higher and higher. THUNK – CLAK – THUNK! Until no end and no beginning was in sight. THUNK – CLAK – THUNK! Only blackness. THUNK – CLAK – THUNK! Every move up the rickety tracks threatened to be the last. THUNK – CLAK – THUNK!

At the apex they stopped and teetered on the brink in either direction for a moment. There was nothing but blackness in every direction, and the tracks seemed to vanish completely on both sides.

In one brief glance, Russell and Jeff shared each other's terror just before the coaster plummeted forward, screaming into the void at breakneck speed.

"*Shiiiiiiiiiiit!*" Their stereo shout echoed all around them as faster and faster they plunged, knuckles gripped white on the safety bar, a collective scream held captive in their throats. But just as the force of their descent promised to pull their faces over the back of their heads, the car stopped.

Jarring suddenness slammed their stomachs into the metal bar holding them inside, and hurled them towards the darkness. Amidst their panic-filled flight, the scene melted and changed again. Where there had been rails, a splintered and bloodstained wood floor reached up to greet their fall, while sparks flickered and popped just above their heads. Two rows of metal bars encircled the area where the track had been, and surrounding them—both men still in the coaster car—were a dozen similar coaster cars, only now they were bumper cars. All were small, dented, scratched, with dull paint jobs and large racing numbers stenciled to their sides. Electric sparks erupted from metal poles attached to the back of the cars that reached up to the hidden ceiling. One-by-one, the driverless cars slowly turned to face Jeff and Russell, small headlights flaring to life to blind the two men.

"Russell, this isn't funny anymore man."

"It stopped being funny a long time ago."

"No man, it's worse for me," Jeff said. "I've always hated bumper cars, even when I was a kid. I always got stuck with the crappy car and spent the next five to ten minutes getting my ass kicked by all the jerks in the other cars, but even worse than that, I especially hate bumper cars with minds of their own!" Jeff clutched at Russell's arm in a panic.

As if on cue, a red car with a large yellow number five smashed into the side of the car next to the two men, and suddenly they were inside a small car, one with no headlight, no pole, no steering wheel and no power, sitting dead center of a dozen angry and possessed bumper cars. Yellow Five slammed into them from the left, rattling their teeth with the impact. Black Seven was next, crashing into them from the right and nearly rocking them both out of the car and slamming their heads together.

Before they could even think of recovering, Green Six barreled down on them from the rear.

This time Jeff was thrown from the car to be sent sprawling unceremoniously across the floor on his face and stomach.

"Jeff!" Russell screamed and stared with a mixture of horror and disbelief as bumper cars driven by invisible hands corralled their prey like a pack of rabid jackals. Dazed, Jeff was barely on his feet before Blue Thirteen sent him careening off the hoods of several other cars in a trail of blood.

Russell stomped on the electric pedal several times, expecting power to surge through it if he pressed hard enough. "Shit!" In desperation, he dove out of the car, narrowly avoiding Blue Thirteen and hauling Jeff to his feet right before Yellow Three would have crushed his head. "Run! Goddamn it! Run!" Stumbling, Russell grabbed Jeff by the collar, jerking him towards the rail.

"Wha...what the hell is..."

"Don't think! Just run!" Russell ran forward between charging cars, dragging Jeff dazedly behind him.

"You must... keep your hands inside the vehicle... at all times." The voice came from nowhere and everywhere all at once. "It's for your own safety, gentlemen."

Without warning, electricity shot down the poles like lightning to dance across the floor and through the men's heels, rocketing them out of their shoes and across the railing.

A trail of smoke led back to their shoes, now burning and melted to the floor.

Falling and rolling, Russell stopped and looked up to see a large, mirrored wall in the shape of a gigantic clown's head, exaggerated smile and all. Pushing himself to a seated position, Russell realized the scene had changed again.

The bumper cars and the corral were gone...and so was Jeff.

Panting for breath and grimacing in pain, Russell slowly stood up, using the mirrored wall for support. "Okay, I get your sick game. If we play along with your carnival of madness, we live. If we don't, well...we don't."

Standing against the mirrored clown and peering into the blackness all around him, Russell raised his voice and said, "That's it, right? Yeah, play the clown's game and this all becomes a fucked-up memory." Time passed without measure while Russell waited on an answer to his challenge. "Okay, so, that's it," he said to himself, reasoning he'd struck a nerve with his epiphany. "Right, let's do this." Slowly, Russell turned to face the grinning clown, and with one deep breath, walked boldly forward, then through the reflective maw. Inside, he found a maze of mirrors covering the floor, wall and ceiling, each casting a distorted and disturbing reflection.

A quick glance over his shoulder and his fears showed exactly what he expected to see—no trace of an opening ever having been there. "This isn't real." Resolutely squinting into the gloom, he moved forward deeper into the house of mirrors, expecting the ground beneath him to give way with every slow footstep. Each turn of a corner seemed identical to the last and the faces, his face, grew nearer with every step. Each reflection stared back at him, shorter, taller, fatter, skinner, older, younger, mocking his movements with their eyes, eyes that followed him as he passed.

Russell did his best to ignore the leering visions assaulting his brain from every angle. Each one was him, or rather, versions of him from birth to decaying compost, and a myriad of combinations in-between. Upon reaching an octagonal-shaped mirror chamber, all the images laughed at him. "This is just not possible."

"Of course... it's possible." The damned voice had returned!

"No, it's all a trick...a..."

"Magicians... do tricks, boy. Do you think... I'm a magician?"

Suddenly, all of Russell's reflections vanished to be replaced by warped images of the clown, the psychopathic laughter bouncing off every mirror and casting physical ripples across the mirrored surfaces.

As the laughter died down, the images faded, leaving blank mirrors surrounding Russell, as if he didn't exist at all. Drifting smoke within the mirrors gently rolled in beneath the surface, leaving a new image in their wake. Slowly, one by one, they reflected images from Russell's life: his mother's bloody death at his birth, the beatings from drunken relatives, his private thoughts, the day his father left, the fantasies of his baby sitter, torturing neighborhood pets with bottle rockets, petty theft, drunken seduction, taking advantage of a fat girl from a frat party he'd attended and the following mockery she'd suffered because of it, her naked body in bath water covered in blood as it oozed from her slit wrists. Every horrid thought, every perversion, every lie, every cheat, and every cruel deed Russell had ever done, considered, or accidentally dreamt of was played out across the mirrors, like a thousand miniature movie screens complete with surround sound, each one asking him, "Why? Why did you do it?"

He covered his ears, the sounds filtering through now mixed with the sickening laughter of the clown. He closed his eyes but the images were still there, spinning in dazed circles, tears flowing, his body wracked with sobs; he couldn't escape himself and dropped to his knees. "*Noooooooo!*" Russell's scream drowned the voices, the laughter, and silence engulfed him for a brief moment.

The only sounds were now his labored breath and sobs. But it would be a short-lived reprise, and as if in retaliation, every image screamed his name back at him, before exploding in a shower of glass, the memories slicing and tearing through his flesh from every angle.

Black faded to gray, and growing at its center was a rectangle of white. Lines cracked across the rectangle, then black with white numbers flipped a countdown from four; then there was the voice. "Still with us... good. I have a new... ah... medium I've been toying with... I'd like your honest opinion." Brown wooden walls cracked with age, and decorated with rusted nails, formed around Russell, who now found himself seated in the roller coaster car once more, a large movie screen before him. Slowly, the car lurched forward, and with each movement a new screen appeared in the blackness all around him. "Art is simple... boy. Pure, raw, from the soul." An image of Jeff's bleeding face came into crackling focus on all the screens, and the car moved slowly upwards. Russell sat still, too numb to react, his sanity teetering on the edge as spittle and blood dripped from his slack jaw. "When I started... I was clumsy... I hadn't yet...ah... came into my art." Jeff's face was replaced by a young woman impaled by a fence post from spine to neck, her arms outstretched to either side. The screen changed again, and this time a young black man was nailed to a wall, his innards hanging from a gaping hole in each hand, his intestines stretched to his chin, as if he was playing a violin with his organs. "I wanted the world... the whole world... to see my art for the... statement it was." The voice grated through Russell's very soul.

At some point the car began a slow but steep descent, threatening to drop Russell's body out at the slightest jerk.

"In each town... I found a new inspiration..." Another young man, this time in an old fashioned football player's uniform, lay sprawled on the ground in a pool of his own blood. His head was removed from his shoulders and had been placed in his right hand, as if he would throw his skull for a touchdown pass. "It all came back to the right setting... the mood if you will." Moonlight shone down on a crude sidewalk painting, the camera panning to a paintbrush sticking out from the stump of a slender arm, as blood pumped down the bristles, a stump attached to a lovely young woman sprawled out next to her life's work. "There was one constant... through it all... can you guess what that was, boy?" Again the camera panned away from the body, following the light to its source — the full moon glowing high above. "She was always watching... the lady on the moon... it's for her I make art." Moonlight transitioned to garish circus spotlights, pointing in all directions at once, then like a shot all light focused on the center stage now displayed on the screen. Towards the center of this circle, Russell's car slowly rolled on. "Things change... yes they do... but mostly it's the people... people change and time forgets."

Jeff's body came more clearly into view as if a camera lens were being focused. He was a shadowy figure at first, surrounded by inky darkness, but it soon parted like a living thing, revealing Jeff in the center light. Jeff's hands were nailed together with a single spike above his head, another through his ankles, affixing him to a large wooden pole. Light spread out, further showing the pole running from the sawdust-covered ground to the apex of a great carnival tent. Across all the screens, Jeff's face showed signs of ruin: slices of flesh hung from most of his skull, one eye stared into oblivion, the other drooping from its socket to stare at the ground.

"The problem... as I see it... is I've lost touch with this generation... as it has lost touch with itself." Double trapeze bars drifted into view high above, swinging of their own volition. Rows of wooden stadium seating formed into being, each filled with decaying corpses. Their dead eyes stared at the scene before them; Jeff coughed and a flow of blackish blood poured down his body with each convulsion.

The image of the grotesque clown, Jo-Jo, filled the screens with a smile of sharpened teeth encased in black gums, his eyes burning with green fire. "You and your, ah... friend... have been a lesson for me... not an inspiration mind you... but a stepping stone of sorts..." Jo-Jo crossed the screens one at a time, and each vanished as he passed. With a sickening laugh full of malice and hate, Jo-Jo walked directly out of the camera view and atop the heads of the audience. "You see... there was a time when art..." Each word was emphasized by a hop, step, or an exaggerated lunge to another skull top. "Ah, expressed itself... you could sense the ah, passion... you could feel what the artist felt..." With a dive and flip belying his monstrous physique, Jo-Jo landed with a flourish directly in front of Jeff's hanging body, just as Russell's car came to a stop at the foot of the stage "Now however... there is a lack of that, ah... spark... shall we say..." A knife appeared in his hand, balanced by the blade tip "No, no spark at all... but you do have a violence..." The knife spun and flew from one hand to the other, over his head, behind his back, then in a final fluid motion he sliced through Jeff's stomach, spilling the young man's entrails across the stage "An ah, appreciation for violence... yes, unmatched appreciation..." Jo-Jo reached into Jeff's body and pulled back a length of intestine, which he proceeded to extract one length at a time, as if measuring it for distance. "Perhaps then, ah... I pose this to you..." Holding one end of Jeff's intestine in one hand and the rest in the other, he let the center mass drop to the sawdust floor. "Perhaps that's the art of this, ah... time." Using Jeff's guts as a jump rope, he began to skip to the macabre applause pouring from the dead mouths all around him. "I think I'll like this, ah... time... I think it's, ah... ready for my return to the, ah... art world... don't you?"

Russell's world spun beyond control, faces leering, merging, laughing, swirling about the demonic smiling clown. His body lurched forward, and he screamed out animalistic, unintelligible words. Suddenly, he was clutching Jeff's bloody corpse as Jo-Jo danced on without a care in the world. Tears mingled with blood-wracking sobs, shaking his body, as the scene around him melted. It all swirled together until their colors became the blackness that had claimed him in the beginning, then it slowly receded, transforming back to the sidewalk, buildings, street, night sky, and finally the neon clown, still laughing down at him as he lay curled in the fetal position, rocking back and forth, covered in Jeff's blood as he held his friend close.

"Only a nightmare...not real...Jeff..." Russell whispered. Tears streamed down his face to slice though the blood splatter on his cheeks, to then merge with the filth on the ground around him. "Oh God...he's coming..." Sirens and lights in the distance came closer as someone walking down the sidewalk screamed. Russell sat there mumbling, covered in Jeff's blood. "Art is life and life is pain..." he said softly. His body was bathed in the glare of headlights as the red and blue of police lights flashed in his eyes.

None of it was real. It couldn't be. Then hands were grabbing him, and there were voices, but he couldn't understand them.

Handcuffed and thrown into the back of a police car, he rocked back and forth, as sweat stung his eyes. "Dear God... he's coming..."

Epilogue

Hours later, after the police and paramedics were gone, and the night reclaimed the street, a gentle breeze blew across the sidewalk as a figure walked towards the light of the clown marquee. There was a bucket at his side, a squeegee over his shoulder, and a low whistle on his lips.

Clancy placed the bucket on the scaffold, closed the gate behind him, and pressed the 'up' button, whistling all the while. Stopping just below the mouth of the giant, grinning neon clown, he dunked his squeegee in the sudsy water to clean the fresh blood dripping from the clown's teeth. "Ah, good ol' Jo-Jo; always knocks 'em dead."

A faint but deep laugh sailed on the wind, and into the darkness of the City of Sin.

TIBO IS GONNA GETCHA

ANTHONY GIANGREGORIO

Tina lay on her bed, staring up at the ceiling, thinking about how she was going to get even with her sister, Lisa.

Oh yes, Lisa was going to pay for what she'd done to Tina.

The two sisters were only a year apart, and sometimes that would cause problems for them, such as when Tina met a boy she liked only to have Lisa steal him right out from under her. Such had been the case last week, when Tina had been asked out by Bobby Damond, a senior in their high school. Tina had been swooning over him for more than half the year, and when he finally asked her out, she thought she'd died and gone to heaven.

But no sooner did her life come into perfect alignment, then Bobby told her that he'd changed his mind and was going out with Lisa instead. To say Tina's world had imploded would have been an understatement. Lisa told Tina she was sorry, that she hadn't planned it like this. It was just that she had run into Bobby at the store and they'd begun talking, and before they knew it they were kissing behind the store, a make-out session to end make-out sessions. The rest of what Lisa said had gone unheard by Tina, who'd become so filled with rage that she had blocked it all out.

For the next week Tina had been thinking of a way to get even with Lisa, but instead of doing something silly, this time she wanted to make sure it was something that would be remembered for years to come.

At first she couldn't think of a thing…well, not something to be remembered for years, but then Tina recalled how much Lisa hated clowns, how terrified she was of them actually.

She thought back to how it had come about, smiling all the while. The girls had been ten or eleven at the time, and had gone to the local fair/carnival with their parents one bright and sunny Sunday afternoon in august.

Their parents had let them go off alone, as long as they promised to stay together, that is, and the girls had agreed wholeheartedly. Then, with twenty dollars that they could spend between the two of them, they headed off deep into the fair to go on the rides, eat cotton candy and fried dough.

They were barely out of eyesight of their parents before suddenly, a giant clown popped up from out of nowhere and squeezed a big red horn right in Lisa's face. The young girl screamed in terror, and tried to run away, but she tripped over her own two feet. The clown, not realizing that he was terrifying the little girl, leaned over, honking the horn some more and laughing loudly. Only to Lisa it was like he was shrieking at her, his white, pasty face, red nose and colorful hair something that she'd only seen in her nightmares.

Lisa began to scream some more, her eyes squeezed closed as she called out for her mommy to save her. That was when a passerby realized something was wrong and quickly shoved the clown out of the way, all the while the clown not understanding what was happening, and trying to explain that he had done nothing wrong. The man who had shoved the clown wasn't interested though, and told the clown to shove off or he would get a punch in the nose for his trouble. The clown, dejected, had stomped off, his red shoes flapping in the dust, the bells on his suit jingling merrily.

Tina had helped Lisa up and together they had returned to their parents, and after sharing the dreadful experience, they had all left the fair that day, never to return as a family again, for nothing could get Lisa to go back to the carnival, or a circus, or a birthday party, if she knew a clown was going to be there.

Tina chuckled to herself as she gazed across her bedroom to the clown doll sitting on her dresser. She'd been walking home from school yesterday and had passed a yard sale. Though it was odd for someone to have a yard sale on a weekday, she hadn't given it much thought, and had barely glanced at all the odds and ends up for sale. But just before she was past the house and thinking of other things, a colorful bit of material caught her eye and she found herself stopping to see what it was that had grabbed her attention.

It was a doll, but not just any doll. It was a clown doll.

The thing was old, that was for sure, and as Tina moved closer, she could see that the red and yellow outfit the clown wore was threadbare, even a few holes here and there. The face, which was once a bright white, was now a faded yellowish color, similar to old parchment.

The eyes, once a deep blue, were now opaque. The red nose that had once been shiny and new was now chipped and had a crack in it, and the hair, once blue and lush, was now thin and wispy, as if the clown had been aging like a human would.

Still, there was something about the doll that grabbed Tina, and the instant she laid her eyes on it, her devious plan was concocted, even before she'd reached into her pocket and pulled out the three dollars the old woman wanted for the old thing.

"Are you sure you want that old thing, dearie?" the old woman asked. "Tibo can be trouble. They say unexplained deaths crop up wherever he's been."

"I'm sorry? I don't understand," Tina said, thinking the old woman must be senile. She handed the woman the money. "I need the doll for something I want to do. It's for sale, right?"

"Thank you, dearie," the old woman cackled, as she shoved the three bucks into an old wooden cigar box. "Indeed it is. I hope you have better luck with ole' Tibo than I ever did."

Tina only smiled in that patronizing way that young people do when confronted by an old person, and as she turned away, the old woman said, "Just be sure not to get any blood on ole' Tibo. If you do, you'll regret it."

"Ah, sure, okay, I guess," Tina said, then picked up her pace to get away from the crazy old woman. Blood? Now why in the world would she want to get blood on the doll?

As she walked, she studied the clown in her hands, scrutinizing it more carefully. There was a larger tear on the back of the doll and she opened it with her fingers, spying some strange and tiny, marks there on the wooden frame. They looked like something from a voodoo movie she'd watched last year. There were five symbols. One on top of the other, each one more unreadable than the last, as they were so faded from time to be illegible. She didn't give it much thought as to why the symbols were in a place that they would normally never been found, and only because the material that made up the doll's suit was so old and had teared were the symbols discovered.

Shrugging at the mystery, and not really caring, she shoved the doll into her backpack, pulled out her cell phone, and began texting one of her friends, all the while thinking about the coming night and how she would finally get even with her sister.

And now that time had come. She checked the clock on her nightstand, seeing it was 10:50. Lisa went to bed around eleven on a school night, and it was only Wednesday. She could hear her parents talking softly down the hall, as they too got ready for bed. Tina smiled again, then yawned, as she thought about what was to come.

The only problem was that she was pretty damn tired, too, and before she realized it, she had drifted off to sleep herself, her plans going up in smoke.

Tina's eyes snapped open at two in the morning, and she jumped up, as if she was late for school. Something had woken her and she didn't know what, but she was glad it did, for as she gazed at the clock and saw what time it was, she realized what had happened. She cursed herself for falling asleep. What an amateur she was. She couldn't even stay awake long enough to plant the clown doll in Lisa's room after her sister had fallen asleep.

But then she thought that the plan wasn't a total wash out, and that she could still do exactly what she wanted now, and in fact it might even be better for Lisa had been sleeping for hours and would never wake up when Tina entered her room.

Tina went over the plan in her head one more time as she got up and put on her slippers. The room was dark but she could still see, due to the light from the streetlight outside her window seeping around her shade. Because of this her room was never truly dark, but she didn't mind.

She had planned to sneak into Lisa's room after her sister had fallen asleep, prop the doll on her nightstand beside her clock, and in the morning, when Lisa woke up and groggily glanced at her clock to see what time it was, the doll would be staring at her, and no doubt the sight of the clown would freak her the hell out.

Slipping on her robe, she went to her dresser and reached out to pick up the doll. As her hand wrapped around its head, she suddenly cried out in pain, yanking her hand back. The light was off in her room, her mother turning it off no doubt, and Tina went to the lamp on her dresser and turned it on. There, on the tip of her index finger, was a small drop of blood, barely there at all.

Putting the finger in her mouth, she winced, her tongue feeling a tiny splinter there. Using her teeth, she was able to get it out, and she spit the miniscule splinter out of her mouth and across the room. It was so small it didn't matter where it landed.

She sucked on the finger for another five seconds, then she grabbed the doll and snuck out of her room, across the hall and into Lisa's room. But her finger was still bleeding, and a tiny, ever so little bit of her blood got on the doll's red and yellow suit. The blood soaked into the part that was red and so wouldn't be noticed, even if someone knew and wanted to search for it.

Unlike Tina's room, Lisa's bedroom was very dark, her window facing the back of the house, and only the light seeping in from Tina's room across the hallway illuminated the space. As Tina moved closer to the bed, she could see that her sister was definitely asleep, and heard the girl breathing softly.

Tiptoeing closer, Tina held the clown high, even waggling it in front of Lisa's sleeping face. She would love to wake her up, and when Lisa's eyes popped open and saw the clown before her, it would scare the hell out of her, but Tina knew the best way was to wait, to be patient. Let Lisa wake up on her own, and then discover the clown doll waiting for her.

Cautiously, not wanting to make a sound, or make a board creak under her feet, Tina moved to the nightstand beside Lisa's bed and carefully propped the clown up so that it was right beside the clock. She even was able to set up the hands so that they looked as if the doll was reaching out to grab Lisa. Tina almost knocked over the nail file on the nightstand, and let out a long sigh of relief when she stopped it from falling off the table. It was made of metal and would have made noise when landing on the hardwood floor. Putting the file back where it had been, which was now beside the clown doll, she ever so slowly began creeping back out of the room, and only let out the breath she'd been holding when she closed Lisa's bedroom door and had returned to her own room.

Before going to bed, she felt pressure on her bladder so she crept down the hallway and to the bathroom, went quickly, and was soon back in her room, in her bed, and under the covers.

She laid there, an evil smile on her lips, knowing what was coming in a few hours when Lisa woke up. As she thought about her sweet revenge, she slowly drifted off to sleep, anxiously waiting for the coming morning, knowing she would be awoken by her sister's shrieks of terror.

Τrue to form, the next morning, Tina's eyes snapped open upon hearing yelling coming from across the hall. It was Lisa and she was screaming.

Laughing merrily at knowing her prank had done its job, Tina jumped out of bed, threw on her robe, and rushed across the hallway, the words, "Ha, ha, I got you for stealing my boyfriend," on her lips.

Their parents were just exiting their bedroom as well, a look of fright on their faces upon hearing their daughter screaming, when Tina held up a hand and said, "I played a joke on her, Mom, Dad, she's fine."

But then Lisa screamed even louder, followed by the sound of gurgling, the screams suddenly cut short.

"We'll see about that," her father said as he pushed past Tina and into his Lisa's bedroom, Mom and Tina right behind them.

Tina, being last in the room couldn't see Lisa, and when she heard her mother and father cry out in horror, at first she didn't understand what was going on. Then her mother began to scream, then sob, calling out Lisa's name.

"I need to call 9-1-1," her father said, and he rushed past Tina, practically knocking her over as he raced to get to a phone and call for help.

Tina was still in the dark about what was happening and the smile on her lips was still there, though it was beginning to fade. It was as she turned to face Lisa's bed, expecting to see Lisa sitting there, pointing at the clown doll in fear, that Tina's mouth fell open and she felt herself becoming dizzy, as if she would faint.

Her mother was by Lisa's side, cradling Lisa in a tender embrace, sobbing long and loud as she rocked Lisa's still body back and forth.

Tina's mouth fell open in abject shock and horror, for there, on the bed was Lisa. She was very dead, there was no question of that fact, as the jagged slash in her throat would attest to. The bed sheets and her upper body were covered in dark blood and the look on Lisa's still face was one of pain and terror. What had killed her had chilled her to the bone, there was no doubt about it.

Lisa's hands were cut and slashed. As if she'd been trying to defend herself from some unseen attacker. But whatever she'd been trying to shield herself from had managed to get past her defenses, and as Tina's eyes shifted and went down the bed, at the foot of it, lying on its back, was the clown doll, its face, as well as its red and yellow costume, now covered in fresh blood—Lisa's blood.

But though this was something Tina found hard to accept, what really put her over the edge was what the clown doll held in its right hand.

It was the nail file that had been on the nightstand, and even as Tina watched, the tip of the file dripped dark blood onto the sheets.

Tina felt herself swooning even more and she tried her best to keep from passing out, but as she stared at the clown doll, the head looking away from her, the doll suddenly seemed to shimmer, and as she watched in horror, the head swiveled slowly to face her, and where the eyes, once opaque from age, and the white paint on its visage faded, now both were brilliant and new. The nose wasn't cracked anymore, and was shiny, and the hair was lush and full, not thin and wispy like before.

Jumping up, the clown grabbed the nail file in both little hands and raced across the bed, up Lisa's legs and then slashed down quickly, the file penetrating her mother's left eye in the blink of well, an eye. Tina's mother had time for one brief scream before the file penetrated her brain, killing her instantly.

Falling to the floor, her mother twitching in death spasms, the clown doll jumped back onto the bed and slowly, while Tina watched, licked the tip of the nail file, its small tongue flicking out and back like a snake's.

Tina couldn't bear witness to the unbelievable scene before her any longer, and she felt the blood rush from her head and she passed out.

The last thing she saw before she slipped into blackness was the clown doll leaping off the bed, and coming right for her.

ABOUT THE WRITERS

Mike Catalano is the author the zombie kids series "My Little Sister's a Zombie by Living Dead Press" "Dead at the Jersey Shore" by Open Casket Press, and "Dropping Fear" and "McCray is Gonna Get You!" by STFU Publishing.

Tony Garcia is a hermit living in the mountains of Arizona. His twisted imagination is fueled by authors such as Moorcock, Lovecraft, Bradbury, and Howard as well as his love of gaming. "The Legacy of Jo-Jo the Clown" is his third published horror story following "Twas the Night" and "Dead Frontier." His next projects include a Super Hero genre tale, Dark Fantasy anthology, and an apocalyptic undead story.

Anthony Giangregorio is the author of 50 novels and children's books, almost all of them about zombies, and has edited over 45 anthologies and books.

His work has appeared in Dead Science & Metahumans vs. the Undead by Coscomentertainment, Dead Worlds: Undead Stories Volumes 1-7, and Wolves of War by Library of the Living Dead Press. He also has stories in End of Days: An Apocalyptic Anthology Vol. 1-5, the Book of the Dead series Vol. 1-6 by LDP, Zombie Zoology by Severed Press, and two anthologies with Pill Hill Press.

He's also the creator of the 10 book action/zombie series titled "Deadwater" and the apocalyptic series "Warriors of the Apocalypse."

Michael D. Griffiths likes to keep busy. He loves camping in the wilds of Arizona , playing poker, and debating such topics as mysticism, creativity, anarchy, and punk rock. In the past, his writing has been published in numerous periodicals and anthologies. He was awarded first place in Withersin's 666 writer's contest. He's the owner of Sharestorm, an online promotion business and he is on the staff of The Daily Discord, Cyberwizard Productions, and SFReader. His "Skinjumper" series has been chronicled in M-Brane magazine and has been released as new novel. The Living Dead Press is publishing two of his book series, "The Chronicles of Jack Primus" and "Eternal Aftermath."

Daniel Loubier is the author of "Dead Summit," and co-author of the Eileen Dietz biography, "Exorcising My Demons: An Actress' Journey to The Exorcist and Beyond." His short stories have been featured in many Living Dead Press anthologies. The story "Dead in the Bed" is his first collaboration with artist and illustrator Brian J. Orlowski. To find out more about Daniel, visit him on Facebook (Daniel Loubier), Twitter (@DeadSummit), and on his website, www.danloubier.com.

Cyberwizard Productions has also recently released his first fantasy novel Dalsala Den.

Brian J. Orlowski is an illustrator and author of two books, "Strange Guts: American Septic" and "The Deific Dozen." His cartooning has been featured in countless magazines and is regularly featured in "Girls & Corpses" magazine.

To learn more about Brian, please visit him on Facebook (Brian J. Orlowski), Twitter (@DrawnoftheDead) and his websites, www.drawnofthedead.com, www.brianjorlowski.com, and www.deificdozen.com.

John Skerchock was born between the hour of man and wolf. During his lifetime he has authored seven books, numerous short stories, several comic book stories, and over a hundred articles. He also edited five books. His favorite hobby is time travel.

R P Steeves is a former teacher and a writer who specializes in the fantastic. His most recent novel, an urban fantasy tale of paranormal detection, "The National Maul" is now available in print and ebook formats, and is the second book in the Misty Johnson series.

Follow his blog and learn of his upcoming horror, fantasy, sci-fi and pulp adventure titles at http://www.rpsteeves.com

Gary Wedlund is the author of the novels "Abi Shaman Within," "Search for the Queen," "The Queen's Return," "The Condotte's Daughter," "Zombies in Our Hometown" and "Atomic Zombies." He is a member of the North Columbus Fantasy/SciFi write group. He has been in several rock bands and shows his watercolors in local galleries.

Gary has served in the US Army. He has a BFA from the Columbus College of Art and Design, broadcast engineering degree from Cleveland Institute of Technology, teaching certification from Otterbein College and MBA from the Ohio State University.

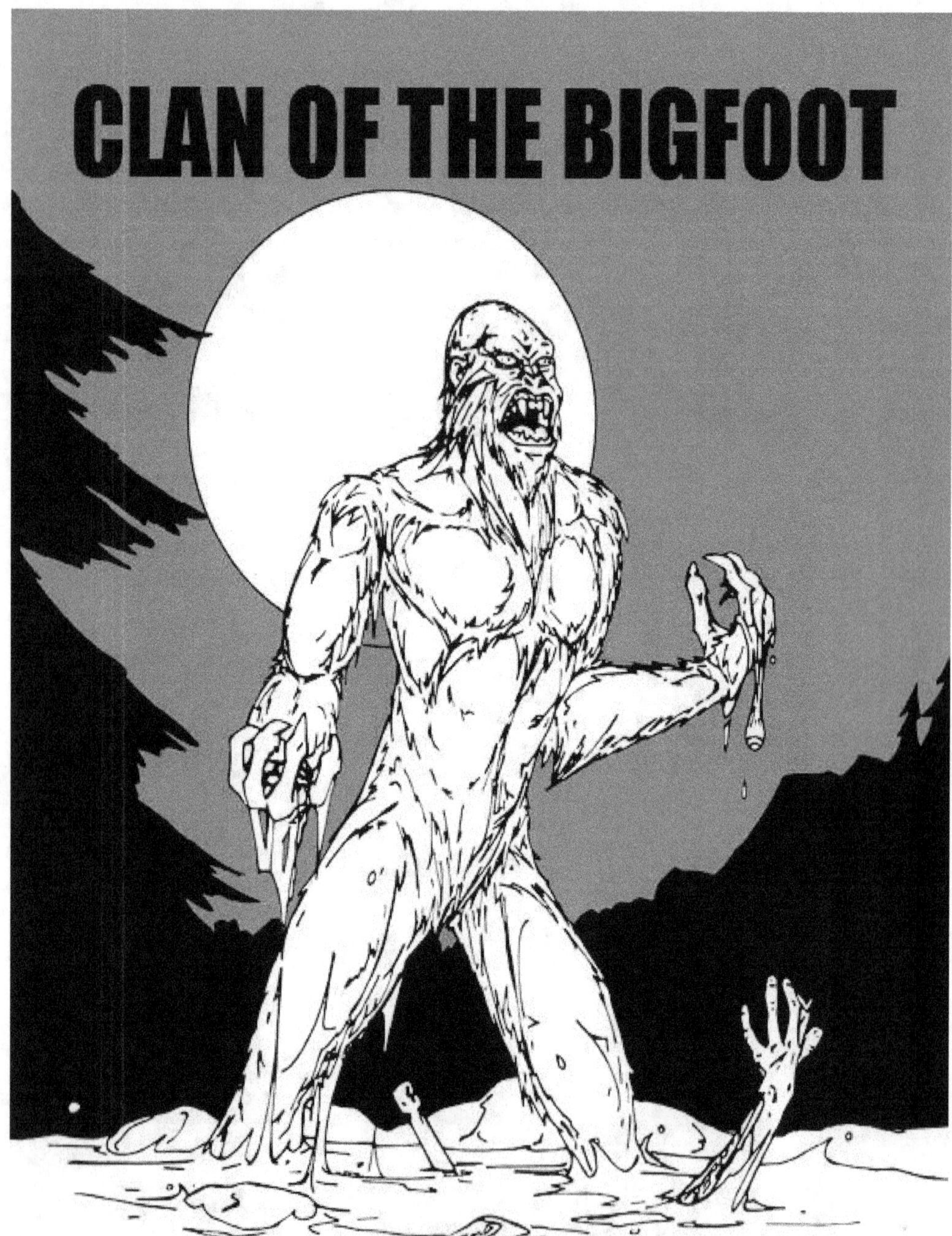

CLAN OF THE BIGFOOT
BY ANTHONY GIANGREGORIO
LIVING DEAD PRESS.COM